THE RICH WEREWOLF

Rachel Esson

CONTENTS

CHAPTER 1

As the trees sped by, Tasha Williams watched out the car window. She sat in the taxi that was taking her from the airport to her new flat in Virginia. The location was warmed by the sun, which was high in the sky. A little after five in the evening, she arrived in the south.

She was excited and filled with delight at the prospect of moving into her new house. Along with her job, she had also acquired a flat.

She saw the sparkling marble floors as soon as she entered the apartment building's lobby. Compared to her previous, modest home, the huge, ornate edifice left her speechless. which, as a result of a gas mishap, was completely destroyed by fire. She was amazed when she saw the location of her new beginning. Her mouth dropped open in wonder as her eyes widened with admiration.

She wondered how she managed to be so fortunate as she stood at her flat door. As she opened the door, she hastily brushed the idea aside. She was astonished at what she thought was the living room's décor. Compared to her prior apartment, it was more opulent.

pristine walls. a tall ceiling and couches in a deep blue colour that appeared to be as soft as clouds. She received the impression that she had entered a five-star hotel.

She continued walking till she saw the door to her room. Tasha hurried over to the room to investigate. When she caught sight of her bed, her jaw dropped open.

The bed was king-size in width. She couldn't wait to squish down into the thick, plush mattress of the king-sized bed. She sprang onto the bed, letting her mischievous spirit take over as the mattress sank beneath her. The pillow-softness of the mattress made her face sparkle with ecstasy as she giggled in awe. She took a look around the space and saw that her bedroom was decorated in sky blue. with a gorgeous bed covered in white silk sheets.

windows that reached the ceiling gazed out over the city. Tasha's eyes were beaming. She couldn't wait to see the scene at night. "Amazing view from a beautiful room. I don't think my life can get any better than this," she declared aloud. Her whole face shone with a smile.

Tasha observed how her room was organised. Across from her, she observed a door that led to a walk-in closet. A door leading to the bathroom was located next to the wardrobe. She was astounded by the bathroom's size and interior when she stepped up to the archway. Not to add the indoor jacuzzi tub. The jacuzzi was next to an upscale-looking shower.

She would never have imagined being able to buy or live in such a property in her entire life. Still, there she was. She was happy and grateful for the chance.

Just as she made a turn to see the kitchen. Her phone began to ring. Without even looking at the phone, she recognised Jade Wright, her best friend, as the caller. To answer the call, she reached into the back pocket of her trousers and pulled out her phone.

Hey girl, how are things over there? Jade welcomed.

"Sis! It's incredible! Tasha replied, "I could never pay for something like this on my own.

At least you enjoy it, I suppose. Anyway, I have to leave. I just wanted to make sure everything is fine and that you got here safely.

I did, indeed. The flight went smooth for the most part. Still not a fan of the landing, but thank God I'm still alive.

"It's wonderful to know. I'll chat to you later, though. I cherish you.

"Okay, girl, you have my undying love. Later!"

The kitchen was more than Tasha could have imagined when she finally found it. The kitchen's brand-new appliances included a microwave, stove and refrigerator. If she had simply judged them by how dazzling they appeared. Marble topped counters were present. The kitchen's elegance was enhanced by the white cabinets and walls. The cabinets and refrigerator, however, were empty. I suppose I'll get takeaway tonight.

Her mouth curved forward into a broad, radiant smile. With the knowledge that she had landed a fantastic job with excellent perks, her body swayed to the song of joy in her mind. It provided her a fresh start in many areas. Despite the fact that she had to relocate a few states away from her best buddy.

Tasha moved slowly back to her room, leaving a trail of footsteps in her wake.

She began unpacking the little belongings she had packed. Not much, especially in light of the fire. She was left with almost nothing to subsist, as a result. She would have been using her meagre money to live in a shelter in New York if it weren't for Jade. If she hadn't seen Jade the week before the fire, it might not have happened. Without any clothes on, she would have fled the building. Having a lazy day that day was really advantageous. She let out a mournful sigh at the loss of the little things she had inherited from her parents.

After completing her unpacking, she placed a Domino's pizza order. She looked at all the toppings and thought, "What should I put on my pizza?" Pineapple and bacon will have to do.

She made the decision to simply look through her Instagram after placing her order. She didn't have a laptop or television. She got a call from the pizza delivery person an hour later, alerting her that her pizza was downstairs.

She said, "Oh thank God, another hour and I would have passed out from lack of food," as she hung up the phone.

Before leaving the house, Tasha retrieved her purse. Before entering the lift, she locked the door. Outside the lift, she pressed the down button and waited.

She was alerted that the lift had finally arrived at her floor by a ding. The door slid open. She was greeted by an elderly woman who grinned as she got out of the lift. Once the woman was totally out, Tasha clicked the lobby button and shut her eyes while she waited for the descent to end.

The front desk receptionist greeted her as she exited the lift. Saying "Good night, Miss Williams."

Greeting her with a smile, Tasha said, "Good night." She was a little taken aback that the woman recognised her name. Her eyes caught sight of Kristy's name in neat script on the receptionist's name tag. Her lips formed a delicate "hmm" as she thought, her head cocked to the side. When she first entered the flat, she was confident that Kristy wasn't there. To clear her mind of any ideas unrelated to food, she shook her head.

Tasha approached the pizza delivery man after spotting him sitting on the couch in the lobby waiting area.

He took the pizza box out of the bag and said, "Ah, you must be Tasha, right?"

She handed him the twenty dollars and said, "Yes, that's me. "Keep making the change."

He smiled gratefully and replied, "Thank you.

"Thank you, too. She said, before returning to the lift and wishing you a good rest of your evening.

She opened the pizza box as soon as she got inside her room. taking a long, satisfying inhale of the savoury aroma. She murmured to the pizza, "You, my friend, are going to be devoured.

Tasha consumed five slices of the huge pizza exactly as she had promised. I should have included a bottle of Sprite with this order, damn.

She put the box containing the additional three pizza slices in the refrigerator. To brush her teeth, Tasha went to the bathroom. She made sure her teeth were white and then had a much-needed shower.

She left the loo with a pleasant grin on her face after about 45 minutes. "Wow, that shower is amazing." approaching her dresser while wearing nothing but a lacy panty. She put on a large t-shirt that formerly belonged to her father after removing it from storage.

I am really eager to explore.

Before she shut her eyes and welcomed sleep, she had one more thought.

Her neck's back hair rose up in alertness. When the predator found its prey, Tasha knew it. She slowly whirled around to face him. He fixed her with those stunningly gorgeous golden eyes. His muscles were clearly visible, and his top half was completely bare. Sweat trickled down his chest in rivulets.

He frequently visited her store. a mystery man who gave her a faceless, lifeless stare. He towered over her by at least a foot.

She experienced a draw whenever he was nearby. a want to reach out and touch him or be touched by him.

He didn't ever speak to her. When he needed her to fix anything on his automobile, his body did all the talking. She had grown accustomed to his hand and head motions. She yearned to hear his voice, though.

He gave a friendly head-up.

Tasha waved while cracking a tiny smile. Even simply seeing him triggered an emotional response in her.

As he turned to walk away, she scowled. Never did he arrive for less than 30 minutes. She wouldn't count them, though.

"Wait!"

CHAPTER 2

At six o'clock, Tasha was startled awake by the piercing sound of her alarm. The sun was shining brightly through her windows when she awoke. Knowing she had to be at work at eight o'clock punctually, she got out of bed.

She walked slowly to the bathroom to take a shower and brush her teeth because she was still sleepy. She would often grab her phone and Bluetooth speaker before using the loo. She sighed at her flimsy motivational speech, "The best way to really wake yourself up is by blasting music and taking a shower."

She finished her duty in the restroom after spending forty minutes there. She moved to her closet while her music was still playing to choose her outfit for the day. She selected a bright pink dress shirt from one rack and a black pencil skirt from another.

She lotions herself with her favourite cocoa butter lotion while sitting on her bed wearing only her dark blue knickers and bra. She put on her day's clothing as her skin felt pleasant and smooth. She then put on her plain black ballet flats to complete her look.

She scowled at the look of her hair while gazing at herself in the bathroom mirror. A month prior, she had straightened her natural coils. when her best buddy and she shared a home. It appeared as though a hurricane had recently swept through it at the time.

Tasha took hold of the comb and started gently combing her way through the mess. She combed her hair sufficiently before putting it up in a high ponytail with the sides brushed in.

She finished styling her hair in five minutes. As she stood in front of the mirror and observed her nicely styled hair in a bun, she grinned with satisfaction.

She prepared herself and went to the kitchen. She normally would have prepared breakfast, but there was nothing in the house to eat. She removed the pizza box from the refrigerator and set it down on the counter.

following the removal of a plate from the cabinet located above the counter. After washing everything off, she arranged the leftover pizza slices on top of it. The plate was microwaved by Tasha. She waited while pressing the one-minute button.

She left her flat after eating breakfast. To get her car's keys, she made her way down to the main desk. She went up to the reception desk.

Welcome to the day, Miss Williams. What can I do to help you this beautiful morning? Tasha was met by the receptionist who smiled.

"Kristy, good morning. I'm doing great. I'm a little anxious. My first day of work is today. Good or bad?

Kirsty gave the new occupant a smile. Her eyes were like a warm, welcome blanket. "I have no doubt that you'll succeed. I'm doing fine, too; I'm just waiting for Mr. Henry to arrive. so he can seize control. I should probably quit work now.

"Thank you, and despite having a long night, I'm glad you're doing well."

"No issue. What then can I do to assist you?

I'm here to pick up my car's keys, but if it's not too much to ask, could you point out where it's parked?

"Yes, Miss Williams, please take this key to your car. Once you leave the building, turn right for directions. Your vehicle was parked in space 130 in Section J.

Okay, many thanks. I appreciate the assistance.

"Thank you so much. I'd be glad to assist. Miss Williams, have a lovely day.

"Thanks. And you."

Tasha left the lobby of the building by going in the direction Kristy had indicated. They had indeed parked the automobile in number 130.

She now anticipated a basic Honda model automobile. But she discovered that her employer only provided the greatest presents for his staff. She was in awe of what she was observing.

She circled around. This has to be a joke of some sort. She was standing and gazing at a 2016 Jaguar F-type. Well, if this is how they laugh at each other. I'd want to see the following two episodes.

She didn't have a long commute to work. Which startled her because she had been waiting in queue for a while. She parked her car in the business lot. Tasha hoped she could park close to the building's entrance. She accidently parked in the space on the second level of the parking lot. She gave herself one final check in the mirror.

She exited the vehicle with a smile on her face and a racing heart.

She walked up to the enormous security officer stationed beside the lift at the Blu Technology Company building. He had a dark skin tone.

Happy morning. She said, "What floor is Mr. Blu's office on.

Do you have a meeting with him today, Miss?

"My apologies, I'm Tasha Williams. I am the new designer, therefore yes, I do.

He is located on the 35th floor in that situation.

"I'm grateful. Have a good rest of the day, Sir.

Derek is his name. No issue at all, Miss Williams. You also have a good time.

Tasha hit the thirty-fifth button as soon as she stepped inside the waiting lift. She tried to relax by closing her eyes. As soon as she exited the lift, a woman was already there waiting for her.

Hello Miss Williams, I'm Miss White, Mr. Blu's secretary. Good morning. Miss White told her, smiling, "Derek phoned me to let me know you were on your way up.

Tasha smiled while her lip trembled slightly, trying to calm her rushing heart. Saying "Good morning, Miss White."

"To your left is Mr. Blu's office. The sole office on this floor is this one. Right across from the lift is where I work. "Mr. Blu is waiting for you in his office," stated Miss White. She indicated Mr. Blu's workplace.

Tasha responded, "Thank you," with a shaky smile.

Standing in front of Mr. Blu's locked office door, Tasha was a nervous wreck. She could only attribute it to the fact that, in her twenty-four years of existence, she had never worked in such a large organisation.

She twice knocked on the daunting door once she had her bearings.

A deep voice said, "You may enter."

Tasha's stomach began to flutter at the sound. Her nerves were beyond normal. She breathed deeply to relax herself. She opened the office door after the butterflies subsided.

Although she had had numerous revelations during her life, the one she was currently confronting was the best.

The man who frequently appeared in her nightmares was seated at his desk and was fixated on her. He didn't move, just like she didn't. However, his golden gaze roved over her body, lighting up every inch of her.

He was seated behind his desk, so she could not view his entire body. But she could tell he was all muscle from his broad shoulders and slightly thick neck. His face was square-shaped, lacking any facial hair, and had prominent cheekbones. He had short curls that had just been neatly clipped and lined up. His dark brown skin was hidden by a dark blue suit.

She fixed her attention on his stunning eyes.

I did not do him justice in my dreams.

Chapter 3

A lexavier walked into his office a little before seven in the morning. He called a few of his clients to inform them he would ship the products they requested soon. After ending the last phone call, he decided it was time to tackle some documents.

His beast was driving him crazy and no matter how hard he tried, he could not focus on the work at hand. At first, he thought it had something to do with the pack due to him being the Alpha. After checking in with his Beta, he realized it was something different.

He knew his Beta had just employed a new designer, and he was trying his hardest to stay focused. He didn't want Miss Williams to think her boss was a nutcase in their first meeting. However, that idea wasn't going well with his wolf acting out of the norm. The poor girl would probably hightail it out of there if she saw his eyes glowing gold.

Just as it hit 7:45 A.M. on the clock, he heard a knock on his office door. From the unfamiliar scent, he knew it had to be Miss Williams. Her scent had gotten his wolf's full attention. He was eager to rip the door off just to see who had his beast's attention. When he told her to come in, he realized his voice was much deeper than normal. He knew it was because of his wolf.

The young lady that stepped through his door had both him and his beast's attention for sure. The melanin beauty standing before him captivated him. Waves of nervousness rolling off her. Yet his roaming eyes had to pick up on the fact that she was biting her lips at the sight of him. He groaned internally at the sexual images that shot through his mind because of his wolf.

Miss Williams wore a black skirt that hugged her hips and a light pink button-up shirt. A pair of black flats covered her feet. This took him by surprise because all the women in his building wore heels. Not that it was required, but he thought the beauty standing in front of him was the type to wear heels.

Her oval-shaped face was free of any type of makeup, and her hair was in a neat bun. His fingers itched to run along her dark skin and his wolf growled his approval.

He could tell that his presence also surprised her. The flash of recognition in her eyes after they widened gave it away. He wanted to know what was on her mind. Alexavier could tell she was trying to piece together a puzzle.

He registered that neither one of them had said anything since she stepped through the door.

Alexavier closed his eyes and took a deep breath just to calm both him and his wolf. Even though quite a few humans were working in his company. None of them knew they were working amongst people that could change into enormous wolves. He wished to keep it that way. His species were a secret among humans in order to keep both species safe.

Taking the lead, he introduced himself to her. "Good morning Miss Williams. I am the CEO, Alexavier Blu. It's a pleasure to finally meet you." A genuine smile formed on his lips for the first time since he arrived at work.

"Good morning Mr. Blu, it's my pleasure to be a part of such an amazing company," replied Tasha with a smile of her own.

Though she still looked a little nervous. Alexavier noticed the subtle change in her body language. The way she held her head a little higher than when she had first stepped into his office. "Please take a seat." He pointed to the chairs in front of his desk.

He watched her intently as she made her way over to the chairs. After she sat down, he asked her some questions just to know more about his new employee.

"So I know my brother interviewed you, but I have some questions of my own that I would like to ask you."

"Um, yes sure."

"What made you decide to be a designer?"

"Well, I grew up working with my father, who was a mechanic. I used to spend my days as a child helping him fix cars. Ever since then, I've been interested in doing something which includes cars."

"That's good. I noticed you used to work as a mechanic before applying here. Why didn't you try for a designer job after leaving college?"

Alexavier watched as she bit her lower lip at his question. He could feel his beast fighting against his restraints at the small motion.

"Um, I actually did, but the CEO of that company wasn't interested in having a female designer. He wanted to make me his personal assistant, so I declined the job. Other jobs required a lot more years of experience in the field."

His wolf snarled at the idea of someone else touching the woman in front of him. This led to Alexavier closing his eyes so he could calm his raging wolf. What the hell is your problem? He thought to himself. He could feel Tasha's eyes on him, but he refused to open his eyes until his beast was calm.

"A...Are...Are you okay, Mr. Blu? I hope what I said didn't offend you?" She stuttered.

"I'm ok, just feeling a little dizzy," he responded in a deeper voice.

"Um, ok, do you want me to get Miss White to bring you some water?"

"No, no, I am fine," he answered. He opened his eyes to reassure her. Alexavier watched as she looked him over to make sure he was actually okay. This made the wolf within him calm.

"What did you design for your final year project in college?"

"Well, they gave us two different car models as our inspiration, which included a Maserati and a Mercedes Benz. I used the Maserati as my inspiration because of..."

How she talked had him very much interested, and it wasn't only because her voice drew him in. Her eyes sparkled as she told him the reason she wanted to be a designer.

He told her what he was expecting of her. Her eyes filled with passion as he welcomed her on board. He knew he had to figure out why a human was calling to his wolf as much as she did.

Someone said, "Be careful what you asked for." The moment Tasha's hand held his hand for a handshake. His amber eyes widened in shock. The depths of his eyes swirled with adoration for the woman in front of him. He had found his soulmate, or his mate for short at last. Just her touch had his alpha beast rolling around like a happy pup, and that scared him.

After telling his secretary to show Tasha around before taking her to her office, Alexavier remained seated at his desk. He was trying to figure out what the hell he was going to do to win his mate's love.

He knew of wolves with lesser status, having a human for a mate. But there was no history of an alpha having a human mate.

Werewolves were blessed to have someone that was made specifically for them.

He remembered the day he'd turned sixteen; the age wolves started to recognize their mate. The disappointment he felt when he realized that his mate was not a part of his pack. Nor was she a part of any other packs close by. Yet the thought of his mate being a human or dead had never crossed his mind.

He'd turned twenty-six years old back in April. How was he going to get her to trust him or get her to accept his world?

CHAPTER 4

asha found it unbelievable to have a dream of someone she had never seen or encountered. Her thoughts were racing with explanations, none of which made any sense. "Maybe I'm still in my dreams," she mumbled quietly.

As she followed his secretary around the building, she noticed a lot of different departments. Her office was on the thirty- fourth floor below her boss. The thought of only being one floor down from him had her feeling giddy. Her mind recalled the feeling when their hands connected.

When his hand touched hers, a small jolt of electricity passed through her, causing her to gasp in surprise. She wondered if he had felt it, too.

Tasha felt like she knew Alexavier Blu her whole life, even though they had just met. She didn't know what to make of reality after seeing the man from her dreams. A man that started showing up in her dreams when she turned sixteen.

As hard as she tried, she couldn't get his amber eyes out of her mind. The light brown color with gold tints to them was mesmerizing. Not to mention the way he smiled at her just before she walked out of his office. She decided it was best to focus on the task he had given her to do. She didn't want to lose her job on the first day just because she was busy daydreaming about her boss.

Tasha racked her head for a new design for the car Mr. Blu wanted her to draft up. However, her brain refused to cooperate with her. She loved cars ever since she was a little girl. The day she was old enough to learn the in and out of a car was one of the happiest days of her life. It was one reason she became a designer.

She couldn't believe that her first task was to design a new body for a car, even though that was the position she had applied for. She thought she would at least go through a week or two of training.

"Mr. Blu must truly trust his employees," she whispered to herself.

Tasha's office phone rang, and she jumped in fright. She was not expecting anyone to be calling her on her first day. She placed a hand on her chest and took calming breaths. Once her heart had slowed to a normal pace, she cautiously picked up the phone. "Hi, good afternoon, this is Miss Williams speaking."

Miss White giggled softly. "Hey Miss Williams, it's Miss White. I am calling to let you know you can take your lunch break at one P.M."

"Oh okay, that's good. Thank you for letting me know."

"No problem, I should have told you earlier, but it slipped my mind."

"That's ok, it happens to the best of us."

"Yes, anyway, I'll let you get back to your work. Bye!"

"Bye for now, Miss White," Tasha said before disconnecting the call.

She checked the time on her Samsung Galaxy S8 Plus. She groaned in agony when she realized she had to endure another thirty minutes. "Way to ruin a girl's hope," she mumbled to her phone.

It was time for Tasha to take her one-hour lunch break and she was glad for that. She was seconds away from dying from hunger. As she gathered her things to leave her office. Someone knocked at her door. When she opened it, a bright smile that belonged to a young lady greeted her.

"Hey, I'm Makayla, but I prefer people calling me Mac."

"Hi Mac, I'm Tasha or maybe you already knew that..." she trailed off, not quite sure.

"No, I didn't know your name. I knew that there was a new designer and that the designer was a woman. So I thought I would come up and say hello. Also, to ask you if you wanted to join me for lunch?"

"Oh, that makes sense, and I wouldn't mind joining you for lunch. Especially since I'm not from around here," Tasha said. A grateful smile appeared on her face.

Mac smiled in return before nodding at Tasha to follow her.

"Give me a minute, let me just grab my handbag," said Tasha. She took her bag out of the desk drawer. Double checking that she had all that she needed.

Mac stood by the door waiting patiently, glad that she had gathered up the courage to approach Tasha. Even though she had been working at the company for years. She rarely socialized with others unless it was work related. Everyone was friendly, but she still felt kind of inferior to a lot of them. Their beauty alone intimated her.

"Alright, lead the way," said Tasha.

They both walked toward the elevator. Something about Mac had Tasha feeling as though they were going to be great friends.

"So, what do you feel like having for lunch? There is a Chinese restaurant across the street...?" asked Mac. She pointed toward the Chinese restaurant literally across from them as they stepped out of the building. "Or... Checkers, which is about a fifteen-minute walk from here?" she questioned with a raised eyebrow.

Tasha stood pondering what she felt for at the moment. "Hmm, I think I'll go with Chinese food today."

Mac grinned from ear to ear, happy with Tasha's choice. "Yes, we are definitely going to be great friends."

Tasha smiled at Mac's enthusiasm. "I agree!"

They crossed the busy street and entered the somewhat full restaurant. They found a table next to the window, and they each took a seat on the comfy-looking white chairs.

Tasha glanced around the restaurant, noticing that most of the customers were in work uniform like herself. She also noted that even though the outside of the restaurant looked pristine, the inside was a bit run down.

The white paint stripping from the walls, and the few pictures occupying the walls had rips in them.

A throat clearing interrupted her observation. Tasha turned to where the man stood. A man who looked no taller than five feet five inches with jet black hair and matching eyes.

"Welcome to Chou's Kitchen. My name is Lee and I will be your server this afternoon. Do you ladies know what you will be ordering, or do you want me to come back after you check out the menu?" He spoke with a thick Chinese accent.

Mac raised an eyebrow at Tasha in question.

"No, we are ready to order," said both ladies. The two women ordered shrimp fried rice with fried chicken.

"So, what is it like working for Mr. Blu?" asked Tasha after Lee left with their order.

"To be honest, it has been an amazing journey. I've been working with them for four years and I have never been happier." Mac's eyes revealed her honesty.

"That's nice to hear," said Tasha. She noticed Mac was elated to be employed by Mr. Blu. This gave her more assurance that she had chosen the right job.

After exchanging numbers with each other. Tasha and Mac headed to their separate offices at the end of their lunch hour.

Tasha phoned Mac from her office to see if Mac could give her a tour of the town. The phone rang twice before she answered.

"Hey, what's up?" greeted Mac.

"Hey, I was wondering if you mind showing me around town?" Tasha tapped her nails on her desk to ease her nerves.

"Yes, no problem. I would love to show you around Ferryville. Show you all the fun places, can't have you leaving because you think our town is boring." Mac laughed at her joke.

"Thank you so much. Just let me know when you're free to do it," replied Tasha. She giggled along with Mac.

"I'm free after work today."

"Well then, after work, it is. I'll send you a text with my address soon. I need to finish up these designs before I leave work," replied Tasha.

"Okay, sure, talk to you later. Bye!"

"Bye!"

Tasha had a pep in her step because of her creative designs. But she was not too excited about showing them to Mr. Blu. She felt like he wouldn't appreciate her designs. "I would never know if I didn't show him the drawings at all," she mumbled to herself with a pout.

With her nerves higher than the Blue Mountain Peak. Excitement bubbling in her chest, she went out of her office to the elevator to head to his office. On the thirty- fifth floor, the elevator doors opened, and she saw him walking out of his office.

She was stuck in a dilemma. She wondered if she should walk back into the elevator or give him the folders with her designs and quickly return to her office. With her eyes closed, she slowly inhaled and exhaled, dismissing both ideas.

Upon opening her eyes, an expensive-looking suit was suddenly right in front of her. Closer than she had expected it to be when she had closed her eyes.

Chapter 5

It was time for Alexavier to attend his meeting. As he was exiting his office, the sweet scent of vanilla mixed with cocoa butter hit him full force. His mate's distinctive scent made him aware that she was on her way to his office.

He yanked the door open with unnecessary force. He pondered her purpose for visiting, yet the sight that greeted him had him suppressing his laughter.

He observed Tasha as she attempted to steady her nerves before she spoke to him. He could sense that she was trying to decide whether she should approach him. With the aim of aiding her in choosing, he took steps closer to her. However, it only seemed to make her more startled in the end.

Her dark brown eyes flew open, a gasp of shock escaping from her lips. He expected her to run away, but she only stepped back and stared up at him.

As he looked into her brown eyes, it reminded him of warm, melted chocolate. They drew him in like a moth to a flame.

He was pleasantly surprised that his six feet five inches frame didn't seem to faze her, like it did to most people. His beast whimpered at the thought that he might intimidate his mate. Even if it was for a brief moment.

She studied his face, as if she was searching for something, before deciding to give him the folder in her grasp.

"These are for you Sir," said Tasha.

Alexavier took the folder from her. He was eager to see what was inside. He wasn't expecting her to finish the designs until the end of the week. With it being her first day, he didn't want to overwhelm her with expectations.

His previous designer took a fortnight for three drawings. Which was one reason he fired the guy.

Blu Tech had a clear policy against employees sourcing ideas from an employee from another corporation—when he had no ideas of his own. The previous designer had broken that rule.

His eyebrow arched at the first image that greeted him in her folder. The car she sketched had a similar body to his favorite car brand Porsche. To make her anxious, he concealed his facial emotions and kept examining her designs. The three designs he checked out showed him she was a highly motivated designer, and that she adored cars.

"Miss Williams, did you know you have until Friday to get these done? You weren't required to finish these right away—" He watched as she bit her lips while searching for a response. "—Finishing early is fine," he said. "But you didn't have to do it in one day." He was trying to calm her nerves. Alexavier could hear how fast her heart was racing.

"Um... I just wanted to see if you like these or not, so I could redraw them if you didn't," replied Tasha with a small shrug.

Alexavier gave a nod to confirm that he heard her. He wasn't eager to tell her if he liked her first set of designs. He heard a growl of disapproval from his inner wolf.

He was already brainstorming ways to use the two first drawings. However, he was planning to reserve the last design for another time.

His business was praised for their perfect cars and other inventions. With Tasha as his designer, the awards wouldn't be ending anytime soon.

"I'll take another look at these after my meeting. That is where I was heading before you got here."

Her shoulders fell and her eyes dulled a little. She tried to force a smile to cover up her disappointment. "It's fine. Take your time. My apologies for taking up your time. Please let me know if you don't like them. I'll create better designs if these aren't to your liking."

Alexavier nodded his head to show he heard her. His wolf snarled at his dismissive behavior towards their mate. He pushed the button to open the elevator door. As the doors opened, he motioned for her to go in first. He pressed the twentieth button for the conference room and the thirty- fourth button for her.

The ride in the elevator was awkward for Tasha. A minute ride felt like forever, with the boss standing a foot away from her. She looked at everything but the man next to her. She rushed out of the elevator as soon as it opened. "Goodbye Mr. Blu."

His personal assistant (PA), Melissa, and Dane, his Beta, greeted Alexavier when he exited the elevator.

His Beta made it clear the meeting shouldn't take an excessive amount of time if everyone was performing their tasks.

Alexavier knew Dane had more to say, but couldn't because of the presence of the human. He shook his head at him, signifying he would converse with him when they returned to his office.

Although wolves in a pack could mind-link each other. Alexavier forbade all his pack mates from linking while at work.

He was going to a meeting with ten of the leaders from a few of the departments in his company. To avoid too much chaos, and to recognize the value of everyone's ideas, concerns, and progress, this was put in place.

He was meeting with supervisors from Finance, Back-End, DevOps, Quality Assurance, Marketing, Legal, Production, Sales, Risk Management, and Human Resources.

Alexavier was delighted with their progress. This was not a common occurrence for these departments. However, he always felt delighted when it occurred.

After conversing with the department supervisors. Alexavier conveyed to them what he was expecting from them by the end of the week. He exited the room with his Beta and PA by his side.

"Get Miss White to set up another board meeting for the next ten departments," Alexavier said to Melissa. "And that will be all for the day."

"Yes, Mr. Blu," answered Melissa as they all stepped into the elevator.

They all got off the elevator together. Alexavier and Dane proceeded to Alexavier's office.

Melissa made her way to her cubicle near Miss White's cubicle.

Alexavier released a sigh and massaged his face after Dane locked the office door.

"What's up with you, bro?" Dane asked. He couldn't figure out why his brother showed signs of distress. The meeting with the group was a success, so his brother's change in mood befuddled him.

"I found my mate this morning," answered Alexavier while looking out the floor-to-ceiling window.

"What? How? When? Where?" questioned Dane. His face lit up with joy. He held back from dancing at the good news. He knew how much his older brother craved a mate.

Alexavier glanced at his brother and smiled at his excited behavior. In the werewolf community, an Alpha finding his mate was an absolute blessing. The Luna was the epitome of motherliness in the pack. She nurtured the pack, and she was the one to keep the emotional peace. The opposite of the Alpha, who provided and protected the pack.

"This morning, right here in my office."

"That's great, Bro. I'm so happy for you. Wait, what do you mean in your office? Who is it exactly?"

Alexavier chuckled at his brother's bewildered expression. "It's our new designer; the one you hired."

"That's crazy! I knew there was something different about her. My wolf felt protective of her when I first interviewed her," said Dane with a proud smile on his face. "So what's the issue? I hope it's not the fact that she's human?" Dane's smile slipped from his face. His eyes turned to slits.

"No, hell no! I'm just shocked that I actually have a mate. The fact that she started working in our company. Brother, it just feels surreal. I'm worried that she may not want me and, with the events coming up, I won't be around to watch over her."

"Oh yeah, I get what you're saying but knowing you. You'll figure something out and you know your family is here to help."

Alexavier acknowledged his brother, but he couldn't shake off the worry. His mate could reject him even if she wasn't aware of the pain it would cause him. He knew how dangerous and unpredictable a rejected wolf became. That was the reason for a law against wolves rejecting or hurting their mate.

"But onto other things. The pack's annual sports event is coming up. What week are you planning to take off or do you want me to do the planning this year? I know your mate showing up changes the routine." Dane sat in one of his brother's chairs as he waited for the verdict.

Alexavier thought about his brother's offer for a second. "No, I'll sort that out. You will be in charge of watching over your Luna while I'm away. I don't want anyone finding out about her until I talk to her about what she is to me."

"Ok bro, no problem. I'll start making the arrangements for the employees' transfers during the event."

The siblings finished up some paperwork while discussing some pack work in-between.

Chapter 6

As the clock struck five, Tasha tidied up her workspace to finish her day. She grabbed her bag, eager to go sightseeing with Mac. As she walked towards the car park, she sent Mac her address via text. She wanted to drive her car home before her adventure.

She drove home with soft soul music and encountered less traffic than expected. Twenty minutes later, she pulled into her appointed parking spot.

Inside her humble abode, she changed from her ballet to some comfy sneakers. She wanted to be comfortable while touring the city.

As she was walking out, she got a text from Mac. Her eyes lit up as she read Mac's text. Her friend was waiting outside her apartment. She dial Mac as she entered the lobby. "Hey, I was just heading down. I'll be out in a minute."

Tasha waved to the receptionist on her way out of the apartment. She noticed Mac's black Subaru Impreza parked right by the building entrance. Her lips curved into a smile as she neared the vehicle.

"Hey girl, are you ready for the tour?" asked Mac.

"Hey girl! I was born ready!" Tasha replied while laughing.

Tasha listened carefully as Mac told her things about the different areas they passed by. Her eyes roamed around in amazement. Every detail stored inside her brain.

When Mac pulled up to a mall. Tasha all but jumped out of the car.

"Well, aren't you excited?" joked Mac.

Tasha smiled sheepishly, but could not keep her excitement down. The sights, sounds, and smells of the new city were a world away from what she knew in New York.

Tasha was stunned by the beauty of Ferryville. She gazed around the town. The hum of passing cars. The chatter of people mingling in the air as she scanned the various stores and places she wanted to visit with her first paycheck.

Mac told her about the town and where she could go to get things she needed without paying too much.

As exhaustion set in, the women released a collective sigh of resignation.

Tasha chuckled and pulled her phone out to check the time. "Girl, it's seven o'clock. I think we should have dinner and call it a night."

"I agree. Olive Garden sounds good?"

"Yeah, it's been a minute since I ate from that restaurant," said Tasha.

After their dinner, Mac took Tasha home. She told Tasha she had to go pick up her son from his nana before it got too late. Tasha was a little shocked that Mac had a child. Mac looked a few years younger than her, but she was not one to judge.

They talked some more while they were heading to Tasha's apartment. She learned Mac got pregnant her second year in college. The guy left right after Mac told him she was pregnant with his child.

Tasha felt her anger rise at how easily a man could up and leave his pregnant girlfriend. Especially when she needed him the most.

"To be honest, I wasn't mad when he left me, but I was so angry when he asked me to abort the baby. I was prepared to confront a man who was twice as large as me. I'm glad that he decided to leave when he did, because it made me much happier than I was when we were together. My son is a handsome little one. I finished college with a degree in business and I have a great job," said Mac. A proud smile appeared on her lips.

"Well, I'm glad it worked out for you girl and you didn't give up when life got tough. He's going to realize that he missed out on a wonderful blessing soon and by then it's already too late for him," said Tasha. She smiled, her lips curling up like the edges of a crescent moon.

The rest of the ride passed quickly as they shared jokes and banter. When Mac pulled up to Tasha's building, Tasha hugged her before getting out of the car.

"Bye Mac! Thanks for today. I'll see you at work tomorrow," said Tasha.

Mac shouted back, "no problem. See you then."

Tasha made her way to her building lobby. While in the elevator, she thought about her first day at work. The people she had met so far were pleasant and welcoming. Something that was not a regular occurrence for corporate companies.

She still couldn't wrap her head around the fact that her boss was the same man in her dreams. She wanted to figure out how such a thing was possible. There was nothing normal about her situation.

Tasha felt as if she was still locked away in a dream back at her best friend's house. She glanced around the small elevator, checking for any camera before pinching her thigh. "Jesus! This is not a dream." Her eyes widened in awe as the realization hit her.

Her thoughts then shifted to her new friend Mac. She appreciated Mac's kindness, especially when she agreed to show her around. She admired how Mac was unafraid to be her true self, even though they had only recently met. In her book, that was a good way to start a genuine friendship.

After taking a shower, Tasha went to the kitchen to consume her Olive Garden's leftover food. I should adopt a dog to keep me company. She thought her home was too lonesome when she arrived there.

At eight o'clock, she dialed her best friend.

Jade answered the phone after two short rings.

"Hey sis, how was your day?" Asked Tasha.

"Hey girl, it was good. What about yours, being that it was your first day at work and all?"

"It was good. The boss seemed nice, and I made a friend. Her name is Mac." Tasha's eyes shimmer with happiness.

At the mention of Tasha's boss, Jade couldn't resist asking about his physical appearance. She knew her best friend would lose the ability to form proper sentences if he was hot. "So, is that boss of yours handsome?" Jade smirked, already picturing the look on Tasha's face.

"He... He... Um... Yes, he is. Seriously Jade!" Tasha exclaimed. She placed a hand on her warming cheek.

This had Jade laughing hard on the other end of the line. "I just can't resist. Anyway, sis, we'll talk tomorrow. I'm about to call it a night. You know how I like to get my beauty sleep," said Jade. Trying to stifle a yawn.

"Right, bye best friend," said Tasha.

"Bye bestie."

The line went dead and Tasha chuckled as she removed the phone from her ear. She slapped her forehead. It had slipped her mind to tell Jade about her boss being the same man from her dreams. "Maybe next time."

She had told Jade about some of her dreams. When her dreams caused her to experience intense emotions or darken her mood.

Jade had been her best friend since they were in kindergarten. They became friends when a boy took Jade's crayons. Tasha saw the exchange and told him he had better return them. She threatened to punch the boy in his face if he didn't return the crayons. The little boy took her threat lightly since she was a small girl. He ended up going home with a black eye.

Their teacher, shocked at the situation, scolded her. But she didn't care. Her father had told her to not sit back and watch someone else get bullied.

Safe to say her dad bought her a small bucket of ice cream that day. Even her mother couldn't hide the smirk on her face as Tasha's teacher told her about the incident.

Tasha's mom, Sasha Williams, and her dad, Kurt Williams, were strict parents. But they did not play about bullying or their child.

CHAPTER 7

It had been a week since Alexavier found out Tasha was his mate. His brother was the only person who knew about her. He had made no move on her yet. But he knew that if he wanted any chance with her, he had to take it slow. After all, if she should accept him as her mate, she would be the pack's Luna or Alpha female.

The thought of her ruling by his side was something that kept his wolf calm. The problem was, how was he to make it a reality? Being the first alpha to be blessed with a human mate worried him a bit. However, he would not let that stop him from being happy with his mate. A union like his would surely make it into the werewolves' history book.

The pack's yearly event was quickly approaching. Alexavier knew he had to figure out what he was going to do with his mate. He sat behind his office desk in the pack-house, flipping through papers as he made preparations for the event. He would be away from his mate for a week. A week that he could have been with her if he had accepted his brother's offer. But he understood that as the alpha of the pack, he had to supervise the planning. He was longing for his mate, but he had a duty to take care of his pack.

Another thought that plagued his mind was Tasha being around other unmated male wolves. He knew human males weren't much of a problem. But his mate was beautiful. She had already caught a few men's eyes. He couldn't imagine what it would be like while he was away. His eyes flashed gold at the thought.

The males didn't have the knowledge that she was now his. Tasha being unmarked and without a ring on her finger would surely have him on edge. He did not want to kill anyone for touching his female. He had ordered his Beta to watch over her.

He knew one wrong move from another male toward his mate would cause him to lose control of his beast. His mate was a blessing. Alexavier planned to cherish her until his last breath.

The games were held in springtime. When the time was not too cold or hot. All of his pack members buzzed with energy and anticipation for the yearly sports event. It gave them a chance to fully use their strength. They didn't need to worry about humans figuring out how different they were.

Alexavier had a wide range of land for his two hundred pack members. Wherever those who had built houses stopped, three miles to the east of that was where they had at least six fields. One field was mostly used for pack training.

The pack also constructed a park for the children in one of the other five fields.

He called the members of the pack that helped with the event planning into his office. They needed to discuss what items they needed for the event. The people that occupied his office included four omegas, two males and two females who were in charge of the equipment and food. Two male elders who were in charge of the fields, and Gamma Shane.

In a pack, the Gamma was in charge of training the pack warriors and security details. The omegas were pack members who helped the Luna cook and clean for everyone who lived in the pack-house. They were also in charge of cleaning and cooking when the Luna wasn't present. The omegas were introverted. They stayed away from the battlefield. Some of them also worked in the pack hospital.

The elders, which comprised both male and female, were the old Alpha, Beta, and Gamma. After handing over their title, they worked as advisors for the present Alpha, Beta, and Gamma.

Alexavier instructed the people who oversaw preparing the fields to ensure completion within three days. Those who oversaw the equipment needed to get started on that as well. It was likely that they would travel to various countries. They needed top-notch and adequate equipment to get through the event. The omegas needed to stock up on more food and water. Wolves ate and drank a lot more after a good workout.

He was waiting for the list of warriors that won't be taking part in the games from his third in command, Gamma Shane. The warriors who weren't taking part would guard the territory throughout the days of the events.

Even though many feared him as a strong Alpha with incredible warriors. There were still a few who still hadn't quite got the message and would try to sneak into his territory when they thought it was unprotected.

A few rogues have tried to attack his pack a few years back during their games. The warriors tied the rogues' heads to trees as a warning to others. Ever since then, Alexavier made it a priority to change the dates of the games each year.

He had also learned that humans had passed the signs that had warned them to keep out. He didn't want humans to find out another species lived in the woods. Which meant he had to place warriors dressed as security guards around his territory.

During the events, the humans at his company were sent to work in other Alphas' companies. Companies that he had shares in. However, Alexavier refused to send his mate to another Alpha's territory. He needed her close and within his reach. He had everything but the preparation for his mate ready. A problem he was failing to solve.

Alexavier's eyes roamed the group in front of him. "That's it for today. You can all leave."

Even after everyone left his office, he remained seated in his office chair. His desperation to find the best solution for his mate had reached its peak. He could have asked his mother for help. But the stubborn man refused to tell his family about Tasha.

Alexavier was afraid he would get his family hopes up just for it to be shattered if she rejected him. His beast growled in agitation at his human's lack of plan. "At least I am trying. What have you been doing other than whining every second like a small pup?" he asked his wolf. He knew all he would get as an answer was a growl.

Alexavier went through different ideas in his mind. Yet, not one of them was good enough. "Maybe I should just send her over to Alpha Jakes. He already has a mate and I'm sure if I explain my situation, he'll understand." He groaned in pain as he gingerly massaged his forehead.

"No, that won't work because I haven't told my family about her yet. My mother would kill me if I told someone outside my family before her."

His frustration boiled over, erupting in a guttural growl as he rose from his chair. He walked over to his floor-to-ceiling window. The view from his office was quite spectacular. His office was on the last floor of the pack-house. It overlooked a good half of his land.

Tall trees getting ready to blossom. Green grass with small yellow and white flowers springing from the dirt, and little pups playing at the park.

"My sweet mate, I can't wait for the day you give birth to our pups," he mumbled while thinking of Tasha. The thought of their future together brought him back to the problem he was facing.

What is the best option? He wondered.

When he thought he was out of ideas and would have to resort to telling his mother. The perfect idea came to mind.

CHAPTER 8

It was Tasha's second week on the job. She was reporting to Mr. Dane Blu instead of his older brother. They informed her that Mr. Blu had to travel outside the state for business. His absence bothered her more than it should have. She tried to keep a cool and collected facade around everyone at work. However, there was some part of her that missed him. She wasn't sure what to make of her feelings toward her boss.

Why do I miss this man so much? She wondered. We aren't even together. I need to get my emotions in check. Thoughts of her mysterious boss occupied her mind. But she did her best to get her daily tasks done.

Dane had become a good friend to her over the last few days. She enjoyed his company whenever he would visit her office. Tasha could tell that even though the brothers shared similar traits. Their personalities were quite the opposite.

They both have an air of confidence around them. Whenever they were around, you could tell. People didn't need to rush out of their way for her to know how regal the brothers were. But where

Dane had a welcoming aurora. His brother gave off a darker, more mysterious one. Just like his brother, Dane stood at a height of six feet five inches. However, he was not as muscular as his brother.

Though their eyes were both amber. Dane's eyes had copper tints, unlike the gold in Alexavier's eyes. Dane's curly short black hair usually brushed the top of his forehead. His skin was a shade lighter than his brother's. His face was clean with not an ounce of facial hair and his cheeks were a bit on the chubby side. But it did not stop the ladies from drooling over the CTO.

Her friend Mac was quite busy that week. Tasha hadn't been able to have lunch with her in a while. Mac had texted her, telling her it was the time of the year. The season in which all employees were preparing to work in different companies. A yearly occurrence that happened while the bosses went on their family vacation.

Her mind didn't focus on the fact that she would go somewhere else to work. What kept nagging her was the thought of Alexavier already married with children. She was in a terrible mood the whole day because of her thoughts.

Tasha had also met a guy named Chris. He worked in the Accounting department. Chris had asked her out on a date. She had agreed to the date with no intention of actually going. The man was cute, but he could not compete with her boss. The days leading up to their date, Chris would show up at her office. He would request for her to join him for lunch and she would. He was persistent, but his constant chatter helped to keep thoughts of Alexavier out of her head.

What Tasha failed to notice was Dane giving her disapproving looks every time he saw her and Chris at lunch. He didn't like the look on her face whenever Chris showed up. He felt like something was bothering his Luna, but he didn't want to interfere without knowing all the details. As much as he wanted to get more details about his Luna and the accountant. The news about their upcoming date shocked him to the core.

The news might have stopped the poor Beta's heart from beating. He was not looking forward to telling his Alpha about his new discovery. He couldn't think of another time in his twenty-one years of living, where he was terrified to tell his brother something. Dane was a hundred percent sure that his brother was going to lose control of his wolf. He could already picture all the broken furniture in their home.

Occupied with thoughts of Alexavier, Tasha failed to notice when Dane entered her office. His appearance had her placing a hand to her chest to calm her racing heart. She stared at him in curiosity. Her head tilted, eyes squinted as she took in his dishevel state.

He looked as if he was seconds away from fainting. It was an unusual sight for her. She was used to his smile. The few times she saw him with a serious expression was when he was around his brother.

Tasha had the sudden urge to hug him. She refrained from doing so because she didn't want to seem weird. She offered him a bottle of water instead.

Tasha gestured for him to take a seat on her plush couch.

She watched as Dane's breathing gradually slowed. She didn't want to question him while he was having a mini panic attack. "So, what's got you so scared?"

Instead of answering his Luna, Dane kept chanting. "He's going to have my head. But I'm too young to die. Oh God! I haven't even found my mate yet."

Tasha was biting the inside of her cheek to suppress the laughter bubbling inside her at the sight of his expression. Her new friend looked like a small puppy who feared his owner's retribution. "Who is going to kill you, Dane?" she asked. Her head tilted to the left with a raised eyebrow.

"No one.... ah! Please don't go on that date with Chris." His eyes pleading with her.

Both of her eyebrows shot up at his request. She didn't expect him to find out about her date with Chris. Are we not allowed to date other employees? She wondered. Is he worried about my safety?

Before she could reply to his outburst. His phone started ringing. She thought he resembled someone that had seen a ghost when she first noticed him in her office. However, when he looked at the caller ID on his phone screen. He looked as if he saw the devil calling.

"Promise me you won't go." Dane rushed out of Tasha's office with his phone pressed against his ears. His rushed words were more like a plea than an order.

She continued staring at the door that her second boss went through. Her brain was failing her. Tasha couldn't process why he would request such a promise.

Before he showed up, something deep within her heart was telling her not to go on the date. His pleading added to her uneasiness.

How did he find out? Did he tell his brother? Will I get fired if I go out with Chris? Maybe Dane has a crush on me?

No, she shook those thoughts from her mind. Chris made it obvious that he was interested in her. Her work contract didn't ban relationships in the workplace. Dane behaved more like an annoying little brother whenever he was around her. Tasha sat back in her chair, her worried sigh a gentle reminder of the anxiety she felt.

Who could make a man as huge as Dane scared to answer his phone?

A question that she couldn't figure out. She knew there was something the young CTO wasn't telling her. Instead of dwelling on her unanswered questions; she decided to just focus on the work she had to complete.

CHAPTER 9

I t was another boring day for Alpha Blu without his mate. He sat in his office analyzing documents concerning his pack's daily needs and their upcoming event.

I wonder if someone at work is bothering my mate. Not possible, Dane would have informed me. He dismissed that random thought so he could focus on the documents on his desk.

His mind was half focused on his work while the other half daydreamed about his mate. He was deep in his work when he felt emotions that weren't his. Alexavier could tell from the intensity of the emotions that it belonged to his Beta. He had a moment of panic, imagining his mate in danger.

His heart rate slowed as he recalled his brother's promise to inform him at the slightest sign of trouble. Even if it wasn't about his mate's safety, he could still sense his Beta uneasiness. Though it would explain the powerful emotions his Beta was pushing through their Alpha-Beta connection.

For a werewolf to connect emotionally, they had to be oblivious to the exchange of emotions or totally out of control. He opted to give his Beta a call to figure out the situation. "Maybe he found his mate," mumbled Alexavier.

It took several rings before the Beta answered the phone. Alexavier was astounded by the number of times his brother stuttered before he could say "Alpha". The idea of his Beta actually finding his mate was sounding a lot more realistic.

"Christ Dane! What the hell got you projecting such intense emotion towards me?" he asked. He tried to act nonchalant, but his curiosity was stirring in his stomach.

"E... Emotions... Emotions you say, Alpha... Alpha?" Dane's words stumbled over each other as he spoke, barely audible.

Alexavier heaved a heavy sigh, aware that something was amiss. His beast was itching to find out if it had anything to do with his Tasha. He paced restlessly with anticipation. "You know not everything is about us," said Alexavier to his wolf.

"Spit it out already, Dane!" he ordered.

"Um. well... you... seeTashahavedatewiththeguyfromaccouting-calledChris," Dane replied in one breath.

"Dane, I'm a werewolf with incredible hearing, but even I couldn't understand those rushed words. Can you repeat what you said slower? Remember to breathe after each word."

"Oh, Lord! Your mate, my Luna Tasha, has a date with a guy from accounting named Chris. Listen, I tried..." Dane didn't get to finish his sentence.

Alexavier's wolf rose to the surface. His wolf let out a powerful roar, its canines bared in a menacing display. The angry wolf had every pack member in submission. Even the members that were at work and school felt the powerful roar. He threw his phone across the room with such force that he felt the vibration of its impact against the door.

Alexavier was so furious that he morphed into his wolf form without a second thought. His fur bristled with rage. His wolf ripped apart most of his office, shredding the furniture to pieces. The smell of destruction filled the air before he jumped through the closed window.

A dull thud accompanied his wolf's landing, and he shook off the broken glass that clung to his fur. He went straight for the woods that surround the pack house. He let out an ear-splitting howl, wanting nothing more than to shred Chris to pieces. Tasha was his and his alone.

The alpha wolf patrolled the territory, his powerful paws pounding the ground as he terrorized a few rabbits. After his beast calmed down, Alexavier suddenly realized that maybe Tasha couldn't feel the mate bond. That would explain why she would be open to going out with someone else. The thought scared him more than if she had outright rejected him.

An unknown force was pulling him towards the park outside his borders. What he saw upon arriving at the park made him stop in his tracks. There she was, his Tasha, in all her beauty, lying in the grass with her eyes closed.

Delighted to be in his mate's presence, the wolf stood there, gazing at her. Her skin glowed radiantly in the sun's embrace, making her look like a divine angel in his eyes. Her beauty completely mesmerized his wolf.

He longed to press his nose against her skin and take in her incredible smell. His beast was urging him to go towards her, but he knew better. As he turned around to return home, his paw landed on a stick. The sudden, sharp snap startled his mate.

Alexavier couldn't believe he made such a stupid mistake. He strongly believed his wolf did it on purpose. When he looked over at his mate, he found she was already gazing at him in awe. His beast stood tall, proudly displaying his powerfully built body to his mate.

Alexavier sensed she wanted to approach him. He could see her internal struggle in her eyes as she wondered if he would stay put. He was relieved that the area where she lay was sheltered from onlookers.

He planted himself in the grass and waited for her to come to him. He chuckled internally at the amazement in her eyes as she stared at his wolf.

Chapter 10

A s Tasha reached for the door handle to leave her office, an odd sensation washed over her. The peculiar feeling made her stop dead in her tracks. She massaged her forehead in contemplation as the sensation she felt abruptly disappeared. She shook off the feeling and proceeded to the elevator.

The look in Dane's eyes as she waved her goodbye to him told her something was definitely wrong.

After she made it home, she drove to a park just a few blocks away. She wore a loose-fitting T-shirt with biker shorts and her favorite white Nike trainers sneakers. Tasha lay in the grass, its softness comforting her as she mulled over her past.

She missed her parents and wished they were still alive. Goosebumps formed on her skin when she sensed she was being watched. She remained still with her eyes closed. Assuming it was probably someone who was merely passing by. She jumped in terror when she heard a loud snap in the woods nearby.

Her eyes flew open in alarm. "What the hell was that?" She searched the line of trees to find the intruder. She felt her breath catch in her throat as she took in the creature.

Staring back at her was a huge black wolf with glowing gold eyes. The wolf's structure was massive, standing taller than her five feet five inches frame. She couldn't recall Mac saying anything about wolves in the area.

She was stunned by the wolf's penetrating, yet understanding, gaze.

Her fingers itched to touch the wolf. What am I thinking? He was likely biding his time to hunt me down like a true predator. Yet the beautiful creature still captivated her, despite her thoughts.

She couldn't believe her eyes when the wolf just sat there. It bowed its head to show her it meant no harm.

Tasha approached the waiting wolf with caution. Her insides bubbling with excitement. She offered her hand so he could give it a sniff. She was certain that was the rule when approaching dogs. The wolf looked at her hand and scuffed. She even thought she saw a glint of amusement in its eyes. She pulled her hand back. "Right, you're a wolf."

She stepped cautiously closer to the wolf, her heart pounding, and slowly extended her hand to rub behind its ear. When her hand brushed against the wolf's fur, she felt a slight shock. She felt as if her body had been electrified, with every nerve ending alive with energy.

The rumble coming from the wolf caught her attention. It seemed to revel in the feel of her gentle caress.

To her surprise, the wolf's spiky fur was soft. She saw a log next to her and went to sit on it. She used her hand to wave the wolf over to her. Tasha marveled as the wolf bounded towards her, its coat gleaming in the sunlight.

When the wolf rested its head on her lap, she felt a mixture of fear and awe at its warm, furry presence. Is this even normal? She wondered as she looked at the wolf's closed eyes. There is no way this is normal for such a wild animal. Feeling secure, she started a conversation with the wolf.

She tilted her head back to take in the warm orange hues of the sunset. "I think I need to visit a therapist if I feel safe around a wild wolf."

She locked eyes with the wolf, its golden gaze mesmerizing her. Eyes that brought back a memory from a dream she had a few years ago.

"You know if it wasn't for your massive size. I would think that you are the wolf from my dreams. You two look so much alike," she said.

As she spoke, the wolf's ears twitched, as if it was carefully taking in her every word.

"Yeah, the wolf in my dreams, body is smaller. The craziest part is when he changed from wolf to man. As if that wasn't shocking enough. The man he changed into is my new boss, Alexavier Blu. Though I doubt werewolves exist."

Although, she had a feeling that it was a possibility for werewolves to exist after meeting Mr. Blu.

"Can you imagine my shock when I walked into the office of Mr. Blu and realized he was the man in my dreams? I began having dreams about him when I was sixteen. He was younger back then, around seventeen or eighteen. When I met him for the first time, I thought my dreams were a sign. The disappointment I felt the day

I learned he already had a family." Tasha whispered to the wolf dejectedly.

The wolf's low, menacing growl made Tasha think it grasped her feelings and was angry for her. But she knew better. Even though she wanted it, she knew the wolf couldn't understand her.

"I guess I was wrong to think such a handsome man was single. Why would he, though? He was not the one having weird dreams about someone he has never met," she murmured. She felt a deep, stabbing pain in her chest. Her heart ached for a man that was already taken.

Tasha whispered to the wolf, her voice heavy with sorrow. "Go on ahead. I'm sure your pack is worried about you."

He growled at her and remained by her side.

"I'm going home now, big boy. There is no reason for you to be stubborn."

The wolf nodded his head at her words before getting up. He nudged her with his wet nose to signal for her to do the same.

She remained seated, gazing at the wolf, perplexed. She could not accept that a wild wolf had nodded at her. "Yeah, I must be dreaming or losing it because there is no way," she mumbled.

She got up when he nudged her once more. "Okay, okay I'm going."

When she reached her car, she glanced around for the wolf. But it was gone. "Well, this day cannot get any weirder," said Tasha.

She pulled into her regular parking spot in front of her apartment. She walked into the lobby and waved at Mr. Henry at the front desk. Her shoes tapped against the floor as she made her way towards the elevator. She felt lighter after sharing her thoughts and feelings with the wolf.

She couldn't make sense of why she felt so secure while in the wolf's presence. But she was thankful that it didn't have her for dinner.

Tasha was troubled by the wolf's similarity to the one from her dreams. She could not bring herself to believe that humans could become wolves. She was certain that such things exist only in books.

Then it dawned on her that she had met the man from her dreams. "No, that's totally different." She groaned as she trekked to the bathroom for a much-needed shower.

She went to bed that night pondering what to do if her dreams about Mr. Blu were trying to tell her something.

CHAPTER 11

Alexavier was relieved that his mate stayed when she saw him in his wolf form. He regarded it as a good sign. Perhaps she would remain beside him when he showed her his world.

He found the behavior of his wolf to be entertaining. His alpha beast was exhibiting puppy-like behaviors around his mate.

He couldn't bring himself to be angry because he had discovered something new about his mate.

It was still surprising how calm his mate was around his wolf. He couldn't contain his laughter when she tried to make him smell her hand. His wolf had scoffed at her. If she only knew, the only time he would cause her pain was when he put his mark on her.

The electricity from her touch sent a tingling sensation through his body, making his insides rumble in delight. He desired to be caressed by her each day for the rest of their lives.

When Tasha started up a conversation with his wolf, Alexavier was just as eager to listen to her. During that time, he learned a lot about his mate.

He was shocked to learn his mate had been dreaming about him since she was sixteen. It explained the look of recognition on her face the day they met.

It was news to him that human mates had dreams of their mates before they met. Not like he'd asked others about their experience when they met their mates. He wondered if this was the way the Moon Goddess helped humans to find their soulmates. It was something that he was going to do some research on.

Alexavier sprinted through the trees, his fur rippling in the wind as he made his way home. His thoughts went back to when Tasha was expressing her thoughts. When she told his wolf that she thought her dreams meant something when she first met Alexavier. But then she learned he had his own family.

The memory made the wolf within him angry once again. He had no idea who would say something like that to her. But that fake news may be the reason his mate accepted a date with another man.

Alexavier had a restless sleep that night. The thought of his mate being touched by another man caused him immense pain.

It wasn't long before the weekend was upon Alexavier. By the time the sun illuminated the sky Saturday morning, he was already out of bed. He was ready to put plans together that would bring him closer to his mate.

After finalizing with the pack for the upcoming sports event. He called his Beta into his office.

Dane's stomach was in knots, his palms sweating. The recent event made him anxious about the meeting with his Alpha. It didn't matter that they were brothers. He knew that an angry male was an unpredictable one.

His brother's reaction that day was a testament to that. They even had to purchase a few new pieces of furniture and a window. He had to get a few of the pack members to clean up the Alpha's office. He was very much scared for his life.

As Dane sat in front of his Alpha, he could see his brother had calmed down. This made him relaxed a bit more in the chair.

"I will be out for the rest of the day, so I need you to watch over the pack until I get back," said Alexavier.

Dane was taken aback. He assumed his brother would be mad at him for what happened with Tasha. His mouth dropped open as he stared at his brother, perplexed.

His mouth refused to listen to his brain. "Are you not going to punish me for not keeping that man away from the Luna?" Do I really want to be punished for something I can't control that bad?

Alexavier heaved a sigh. "I don't think you could stop her. I found out why she accepted his request."

Dane raised one eyebrow, his expression questioning.

Alexavier's eyes crinkled as he chuckled, fondly recalling the memory. "I met her as my wolf two days ago. I learned a few things about her and why she is going out with that guy."

"What's the reason?" Dane's eyes lit up with curiosity as he asked the question.

Alexavier let out a deep groan and ran his hand over his face. "She heard that I'm already married."

The Beta let out a loud, booming laughter. He settled down when Alexavier glared at him. "Who would tell her that?"

"That's what I want to know too, but she didn't mention a name."

Dane's brow furrowed as he nodded, deep in thought. He knew that the only three people his Luna interacted with were him,

Chris, and Makayla. He couldn't recall anyone else having personal conversations with Tasha. If he had to place a bet, he would bet that Makayla was the culprit. He couldn't see Tasha talking to Chris about another dude.

"So about you taking care of the pack while I'm out for the day," Alexavier said with a raised brow.

Dane's curiosity was sparked. He wanted to know where his brother was going. But he knew better than to ask, especially if his brother didn't tell him upfront. He is probably going to visit his mate. "Sure Alex, anything else?"

"Yes, get one of Sofie's nanny to get her ready by three o'clock. She will accompany me."

Dane stared at his brother, hoping for more information. What was Alexavier planning to do for him to want to bring their little sister along? He didn't dare open his mouth to ask that question. "Alright, I'll get that done," Dane said.

Alexavier's lips curved in a smirk as curiosity swirled in his little brother's eyes. He leaned forward in his chair. "You're dismissed."

His lips set in a small pout, the Beta saluted his brother and exited the office. He jogged over to his parent's house to inform his little sister and her nanny about the Alpha's request.

Alexavier continued working on documents regarding the pack until it was time for him to get ready. He made his way to his room and went straight to his bathroom to take a shower.

Alexavier leaned against his 2018 S class Mercedes, waiting for Sofie.

He had on a black Nike v-neck and skinny black jeans. A pair of white Nike Air force 1 covering his feet.

Sofie joined him a while later. She was wearing a white graphic tee and ripped blue jeans. Her white Adidas high tops cover her feet. Her black coils formed a crown around her oval face.

They climbed into his car, and he drove to their first destination.

It had been a while since Alexavier chilled with his little sister. He was always grinding.

The only occasion his entire family was together was during mealtime. Obligations as CEO and Alpha prevented him from spending more family time.

He knew what he was about to do was childish. But he had no other way to keep tabs on his mate while she was out with another man. Protecting his mate was his duty, and he was going to do it at all costs.

He was ready to stir up some trouble, and he had brought his partner in crime.

Chapter 12

Tasha found herself walking towards the woods. She couldn't recall how and when she got there. An unseen force seemed to be calling to her. She glances up at the night sky. She smiled, taking in the sight of the moonbeams streaming through the trees. The bit of light was just bright enough to make out her surroundings. With each step she took, the force seemed to grow in intensity. She wondered what could make her leave the comfort of her bed and ventured into the darkness.

After thirty minutes of walking, she stopped. She stood in a wide, open space surrounded by trees. The moonlight bathed the area in a comforting, warm light.

Flickering fireflies lit up the night, creating a magical atmosphere. Her eyes darted around, looking for whatever was making her feel so drawn to the place. When she found it, a soft gasp escaped her lips in surprise.

Laying a few feet from her was her wolf. She wondered if he had heard her approaching. The wolf remained laying down and didn't seem to care that she was there. His head tilted up, and she figured he was staring at the moon.

Even though she was reluctant to disturb him, she was eager to know why she was there. Before she had an opportunity to get his attention, he stood and moved closer. She reached out her hand to run her fingers through his fur.

Her concentration was disrupted when she heard the sound of something cracking. She held her breath, her skin prickling as she looked around for signs of another wolf. One wolf she felt she could handle, but she wasn't sure if she could manage seeing a second one.

Her thoughts were elsewhere, causing her to not notice her wolf's absence. Instead of her eyes meeting her wolf's body. Her eyes met the body of Alexavier, kneeling in its place. She couldn't move or speak, the shock numbing her senses. Just seconds before, her wolf was standing in front of her. She was certain her hand was in his fur, so why was her unfeeling hand now on the person she called boss?

When she realized what was going on, she snatched her hand away like it had been scorched. Wait a minute, skin? Taking a deep breath, she closed her eyes and opened them again. Tasha found him standing there in all his naked glory. Her fingers still hummed from the sensation of touching him. It took her brain a moment to realize it.

She hadn't noticed that he had closed the distance between them until she felt his breath on her face. His hand was rough yet tender as he brushed her cheek with his fingertips. She felt a shiver go down her spine as the tingles spread over her skin.

She caught the look of amazement in his eyes. He must be wondering why she hadn't run when he transformed from wolf to man. She was hesitant to tell him that this wasn't the first time she had seen him do that. Her dreams had been about that ever since she moved to Virginia.

When he looked at her, his eyes lingered on her lips before flicking back to her eyes as if seeking approval. She licked her lips, her skin tingling with anticipation.

There was a satisfied rumble emanating from his chest, indicating his approval with her action. She was jarred back to reality when she felt the firm pressure of full lips on her own. Her eyes closed instantly. She didn't think the tingles could get any more intense. But man, was she wrong.

She ran her fingers across his chest, feeling the hardness of his muscles beneath her touch. She wounded her arms around his neck as he deepened the kiss. Her fingers danced along the back of his neck, playing with the soft hair. She was rewarded with a low, throaty growl from him.

Her body shuttered when she felt his member rubbing against her tin pajama shorts. Her soft moans filled the air. Heat pooled between her thighs at his touch.

He let out a low growl as he effortlessly lifted her. She instinctively wrapped her legs around his waist.

When she felt the pressure of the tree at her back, she involuntarily arched towards him. As his lips parted from hers, she started to protest. But the words died on the tip of her tongue.

He trailed open mouth kisses down to her neck. The moment his lips made contact with the area between her neck and shoulder, she let out a breathless moan.

Tasha felt a shiver run through her body as his hands started exploring, only to be interrupted by the sound of her alarm. With a desperate prayer that it wasn't all a dream, she opened her eyes slowly. It couldn't be.

The sensation of her legs trembling was unmistakable as she laid there. She was absolutely sure that her panty was soaked. She groaned in frustration and hit the off button on her phone, silencing the blaring alarm.

Getting out of bed, she felt the cold air on her skin as she removed her t-shirt and panty before heading right to the shower. She needed a cold shower after the dream she had.

After she showered, she brushed her teeth. She got dressed in a simple white v-neck blouse and black joggers. Her feet padded softly on the floor as she made her way to the kitchen to cook breakfast.

When she left her apartment to go to the mall, the sun was already high in the sky. She needed to pick up some more formal and semi-formal apparel, plus new shoes.

Even though the mall was bustling with people, she easily navigated her way to the items she needed.

When she arrived back at her apartment, her limbs felt heavy and her eyes were drooping with exhaustion. Shopping was especially annoying to Tasha because of this. She spent an hour unwinding in the living room. It took her body succumbing to sleep for her to recognize the fatigue that had been building.

Two hours had passed by the time she stirred from her nap and opened her eyes. Despite her desire for a few extra minutes of sleep, she got up and put her shopping away. Organizing everything neatly in its rightful place.

At around six in the evening, Tasha began getting dressed for her date with Chris. She wasn't all too excited about it. Since she'd said yes to going out with him, she made an effort to look decent.

Gazing at her reflection in the standing mirror, she admired her new outfit. She had on dark blue skinny jeans with a white off-the-shoulder blouse and white pumps. Her hair was styled in a ponytail and the tips were curled. She did her makeup light. Her dark brown eyes were enhanced with black eyeliner and dark red lipstick adorned her lips. She wasn't one to brag, but she couldn't deny the truth. "Damn I look hot."

As she reached for her purse, her phone started to ring with a call from Mr. Henry. She tapped her finger against the smooth glass of her phone to accept the call. Mr. Henry told her that a young man named Chris was downstairs waiting for her.

"Tell him I am on my way down. Thanks for informing me."

Chris was standing by his car, the sound of crickets chirping in the background, as he waited for Tasha to arrive. He could feel his hands shaking, but he knew that everything was going to go as planned. Though he wouldn't call himself a player, he had the confidence and charisma to attract women. He was confident he would have her in his bed by nightfall.

The sound of clicking heels made Chris glance up and he saw a stunning figure walking towards him. His jaw dropped when he realized it was Tasha.

She was breathtaking, and her jeans showed off her curves. The heels she had on made her legs appear longer. His hands ached to explore every inch of her body.

"Um. Are we ready to go or are you just going to stand there with your mouth wide open and stare at me?" Asked Tasha the minute she got closer to him. Her skin tingled with a fiery sensation as it ran up her spine. She realized it was not from Chris's gaze, yet she couldn't determine what caused that sensation. The feeling reminded her of the first day she stepped into Mr. Blu's office.

"Huh?... Right... Right.. Right, yes um. Yes, let's go. By the way, you look gorgeous," replied Chris.

"Thanks and you don't look too bad yourself," answered Tasha.

As soon as he unlocked the car, she hopped in. His car had a dark red interior that was pleasing to the eye. She had to admit that it was very much his style.

The car ride was quiet, with only the sound of the engine humming in the background.

She could feel his eyes lingering on her body a few times. She watched from the corner of her eye as his mouth opened and closed in a silent stammer. Failing to get his words out.

With a deep sigh, Tasha silently prayed for the date to end, even though it had only just begun.

A traditional Mexican style building greeted them twenty minutes later, the smell of spices wafting through the air. She was now bursting with excitement and anticipation of the savory Mexican food she was about to indulge in.

Chapter 13

Alexavier parked a few houses away from Tasha's place. He filled Sofie in on why they were there. He gave her a breakdown of his plan.

"You better take me to get ice cream after all this. I do not work for free," said Sofie. "I can't wait to meet my sister-in-law." Her delicate face lit up with a gentle smile. Mischief twinkled in her amber-colored eyes.

Alexavier rolled his eyes, but his mouth quirked up into a tiny smile. "Sure, just don't go overboard with that creative mind of yours and scare my mate away."

Sofie's head was spinning with a flurry of creative ideas. She wanted to give Chris a fright that he would never forget. It was rare for her elder brother to request help from her. So she was determined to make him proud.

Alexavier averted his gaze from his sister, who had a creepy smile on her face. He could smell Tasha's sweet and distinct scent as soon as she stepped out of the apartment building. The pumps she wore made her legs look longer. He felt his dick stir as he imagined her curves brushing against his body.

His fingers tingled with anticipation as he yearned to touch her. All his thoughts ceased when he saw the intense way Chris was gazing at his mate. The low, menacing growl that emanated from his lips shook his sister out of her daydream.

He could feel his beast clawing from within, desperate to break free. His rage boiled over when he saw another male look at what was his with a glint of want in his eyes. His wolf wanted to annihilate the human. Alexavier tried to suppress his growls so that his mate wouldn't notice him.

He kept his eyes on Chris's car, trailing it from a safe distance. Twenty minutes later, he noticed the car pull into the lot of a Mexican restaurant. He kept going up the street until he saw an available parking space at a liquor store.

While waiting in the car, he went over the plans with his sister. He reversed out of the parking lot after checking she knew what to do. It was a short ride back to the Mexican restaurant.

The siblings exited the car. Alexavier made his way around the car to meet his sister. As they made their way into the restaurant, Sofie took hold of her brother's hand.

Alexavier's eyes darted around the restaurant, searching for his mate amongst the chatter of conversation. He wanted to sit at a table nearby her.

"Er... Good evening Mr. Blu. I will show you to your table," said the hostess at the door.

Turning towards the voice, Alexavier read her name tag before replying. "Good evening Jenny. Thank you."

Jenny's cheeks flushed a deep red as she guided the guest to their table for the evening. Everyone in town knew about the Blu family. They would come to this Mexican restaurant at least once a month. The hostess quickly scurried to the door after informing them that their waiter would be with them soon.

Alexavier was aware of his mate's gaze as he took his seat. Instead of making eye contact with her, he quickly grabbed the menu. His eyes darted over the selections as he considered what to order.

Sofie sat across from him, her face split in a wide, victorious smile — like a madwoman who just won the lottery. He considered if he had done the right thing by bringing his ten-year-old sister.

Taking his eyes off the menu, he saw his mate biting her lips while watching him. He rose from his seat, a devilish smirk playing on his lips, and headed towards Tasha and Chris's table.

"Good evening Miss Williams, Chris," greeted Alexavier. "Nice of you to show Tasha around." The smirk remained on his face as he stared at the other guy.

"Good evening Mr. Blu," replied Tasha. Trying her best not to giggle at his sly remark towards Chris.

"Uh... I'm not showing her around, boss. It's more like we're on a date," Chris clarified.

Alexavier was about to make a remark when he felt a gust of air as Sofie skipped by. She Skid to a stop next to Chris.

"OMG! It's... it's... It's Chris Hemsworth! Like the Chris Hemsworth!" Sofie exclaimed with an exaggerated gasp.

"Uh... Um... No, I'm not that Chris." Chris looked slightly uncomfortable with the way his boss's younger sister was looking at him.

"Oh! I really need to get my eyes checked out. This is the second time I have mistaken someone for my boyfriend's daddy," said Sofie. Her shoulders slumped and a sigh of disappointment escaped her lips.

Alexavier was trying hard not to laugh at his little sister's acting. Glancing at his mate, her eyes twinkling with amusement at Chris's predicament.

With a quick nudge from Sofie, Chris made room for her as she sat beside him. She started telling him about her boyfriend being Chris Hemsworth's son. "I've never met my boyfriend's dad because he is famous and all. That's why I thought I got lucky today when I saw you. But I should've known better because my boyfriend told me his dad was on tour for his new movie." Her smile brightened as she told him her fake story.

Chris didn't know how to respond after his boss's sister said all that. He wanted them out of the way so he could keep impressing Tasha. He was trying not to be a jerk. While Sofie continued to talk a mile a minute, he tried to hide his irritation from his face.

Alexavier fought to keep his face emotionless, though a smirk threatened to break free from his lips. Warmth spread through his right hand when his mate touched it, sending tingles up his arm. When he glanced her way, she pointed to the space beside her—inviting him to sit.

"Thank you for the offer. I was wondering when someone was going to notice me standing like a statue and offer me a seat," said Alexavier. He smirked, and his eyes glinted with humor.

Tasha emitted a gentle, melodic laugh. "Your table has enough seats waiting for you. You should just go back to your table if you are tired of standing. Don't you see your daughter has found a date and left you?"

His voice held a hint of amusement as he corrected her. "Sofie is my little sister. I do not have any children of my own as yet. My table is lonely now. I'll go there if you'll join me."

Tasha looked at him and then shifted her gaze to the man she was on a date with. Hoping she didn't have to spell it out.

Chris had had enough of the chatty mouth girl beside him. Exhaling a deep sigh, he slowly faced his date, whose gaze had already settled on him. His silence did not seem to faze her, the air heavy with her indifference. He found her indifference odd because women normally beg for his attention.

Alexavier could see the subtle shift in Chris's body language, a sign that the man wanted to leave. However, the man didn't know how to get out of the bind they put him in. Alexavier turned to his little sister, his expression conveying it was time to leave.

Sofie released a soft sigh. "I guess it's time we return to our table, brother. We haven't ordered our food yet. Let us leave these two to their date."

"Ah, yes Sofie. Miss Williams, it was nice seeing you tonight. Chris, enjoy the rest of your night," said Alexavier.

Rushing to get up, Sofie clumsily knocked over Chris's wine glass.

Chris felt the red liquid splash onto him, followed by the sound of glass breaking. He angrily backed away, glancing down at his ruined light blue shirt and khaki pants. His green eyes were like daggers as he turned to Sofie, and she whimpered in fear.

"Look what you did, you clumsy little chatty mouth brat!" Chris shouted.

His outburst caused the other customers to halt their lively chatter, filling the room with a tense silence. People craned their necks to get a better look. The sound of murmuring rising in the air as they wondered what the commotion was about. A few of the waiters rushed to get their manager. Fearing that the situation would escalate.

Alexavier's face contorted in rage, and a low growl escaped his lips in response to what Chris said about his little sister. Before he could grab the man, he felt a rush of wind as his mate shot up from her seat.

She walked past Alexavier to get to Sofie, shielding her from Chris's gaze. With her right hand tightly clenched, she punched him square in the nose.

The customers' faces showed their shock as they audibly gasped. The manager rushed over to the group, trying to ease the tension in the air.

Chris let out a startled cry as he felt the searing pain of his date's unexpected punch. "You fucking bitch! You better find your way home, because I'm fucking out of here." His voice had a sharp edge to it, poisonous with anger.

"I would rather walk than to get back in a car with such a cretin like you. And for the record, I always walk with my get vex money. So do us all a favor and bounce," Tasha replied calmly. Her fists were clenched, her blood boiling as she thought about punching him again.

Alexavier was seething with rage. Wanting to pummel the guy for his disrespectful words toward his mate and younger sister.

He felt a swell of pride as he watched his mate stand her ground and protect both herself and his sister.

Chris stormed out of the restaurant, his face red with anger.

"Sorry about the trouble we caused," said Tasha to the red face manager.

The manager shook his head at her. His eyes were wide with fear after looking at the stoned face of Alexavier. "It's fine Miss. No one ended up in the hospital." His attempt to give her a smile resulted in a grimace.

After Chris left, Tasha made a step to head out of the restaurant. She was about to order an Uber to take her home.

Alexavier grabbed her wrist to stop her. His touch left a trail of goosebumps along her arm. She turned her gaze towards him, her eyes conveying her silent inquiry.

"You can join us for dinner," he said with a genuine smile.

Sofie stood beside him, her face creasing in a delighted smile—agreeing with her brother.

For the rest of the evening, the three talked about everything and anything age-appropriate while they ate dinner.

"How are you enjoying Ferryville so far?" Asked Sofie.

"It's nice and peaceful. The people here are welcoming," replied Tasha with a small smile.

"I know it's a lot busier in New York than here," Alexavier chimed in.

"Yes, it is, but I like the calming atmosphere. Do you travel to the Big Apple a lot?"

"Yes, when I have business there," answered Alexavier.

Sofie turned to Tasha with a mischievous twinkle in her eyes. "Do you enjoy working with my brother? I hear he can be very intimidating."

Alexavier grumbled and stared daggers at his sister. His glare softened at the sound of his mate's soft giggles.

"I don't find him intimidating and yes, I enjoy working with him."

Alexavier gave his sister a cheeky grin, and she responded by sticking her tongue out.

The evening continued with Sofie asking Tasha silly questions and teasing her brother.

Alexavier was happy that he got to have dinner with his mate that night. He loved that his mate and sister got along. They would even gang up on him some time. But he was good with that, as long as the smile remained on his mate's face.

After dinner, Alexavier took Tasha home, even though he didn't want to be away from her.

He was aware he had to inform her of everything before he could have his mate the way he desired.

CHAPTER 14

Tasha stood at the threshold of her living room, her eyes fixed on Alexavier. The only garment on her body was her lace panty. She licked her dry lips as she took in the way his back muscles flexed each time he moved.

A mischievous smile made its way onto her lips as she approached him unannounced. She laughed at the way his breath hitched the moment she pressed her hardened nipples against his back. The kiss she planted on his back sent a tingling sensation through her lips.

"How long is that going to take?" She whispered with her cheek pressed against his muscular back. She giggled when all he could manage was a quiet growl. That is enough distraction, she thought as she turned to walk away from him.

She gasped in shock as his powerful arms encircled her waist. The embrace of her lover felt safe and comforting as she felt his broad chest against her back. His dick pressing into her lower back. She shivered as his warm breath tickled her neck when his lips touched her skin.

"Mine!" His growl was low and fierce, conveying his possessiveness. His sharp canine teeth grazed her soft skin, leaving behind a slight sting.

The possessive tone of his words surprised and aroused her. "All yours," she agreed, biting back a moan.

She quivered against him, and he smirked against her skin, enjoying her reaction. He cupped her breasts in his palm, pinching and massaging them. He licked the sensitive area on her neck that he knew would drive her crazy. Her moans filled the air, her melodic voice trembling with desire.

Tasha almost came undone at his sensual torture. Her back arched and head tilted to give him better access. The room was filled with the sweet, sultry sounds of her pleasure.

The scent of her arousal almost sent Alexavier over the edge. His dick twitched, eager to satisfy his little vixen needs. He let out a low, throaty growl that reverberated through his chest.

She felt the warmth of his lips on hers as she turned her face to meet his. His kiss was raw and passionate, sending shivers of pleasure through her. He pulled away from the kiss and spun her around, their faces close and their chests flush. His eyes glowed a brilliant golden hue, signaling the presence of his wolf.

As much as he desired to ravish her, he felt himself move slowly, savoring every touch. His lips tickled her face as he peppered her with soft, feather-like kisses. A kiss to her forehead, one on each eyelid, and a kiss to the tip of her nose. He cupped her face with his hands as he captured her lips, and a soft sigh of delight escaped her lips.

He slowly pulled away from her lips, lifting her off the ground and into his embrace. She instinctively wrapped her legs around his waist. Her fingernails digging into his shoulder. He captured one of her nipples in his mouth, sucking and pulling while kneading the other.

"Alexavier," she moaned. She reveled in the pleasure, her eyes closed and her head thrown back in ecstasy.

His tongue licked and swirled around each of her sensitive buds before releasing them. He slipped a hand between her thighs and rubbed over her wet panty.

He felt her trembling, and he growled, loving how she reacted to his touch. Just as he slipped a finger between her wet folds...

Alexavier was jolted awake by the shrill sound of his alarm. He groaned in frustration before trudging to the bathroom and turning on the cold shower.

A dream was something he hadn't had in years. So he assumed the one he had had to be related to him finding his soulmate. A sign that their bond was growing.

An hour later, he got dressed in a white v-neck, dark blue jeans and Adidas slides. He sat in his office, trying to figure out how he was going to carry out his plan. He knew he couldn't just expect his mate to agree to his weird request. When an idea suddenly popped into his mind, he lowered the wall in his mind that blocked mind-linking with the pack members.

"Good morning everyone," greeted Alexavier.

"Good morning, Alpha," greeted all the members.

"We have an emergency meeting in the next half hour. Everyone should be present." Alexavier cut the link before the members could start asking questions. He could feel their confusions and worries at his impromptu meeting.

Alexavier's brow rose when he detected the distinct smell of his brother nearing his office door. "Come in," he called before his brother got the chance to knock. He relaxed into his chair as his brother walked into the room.

Dane bowed his head in a sign of respect to his brother. He settled into one of the chairs. He folded his hands, crossed his chest, and stared at his brother. His eyes studied his Alpha, trying to figure what he was up to.

"What can I help you with, Beta? I know you didn't come in here to just stare at my handsome face?" Alexavier's eyes widened as a thought hit him. "Did mom send you here to find out what the emergency is?"

Dane clicked his tongue as he unfolded his hands, a smirk forming on his lips. "No, I left the house before she could question me about something only you knew."

With a sigh of relief, Alexavier eased into the comfort of the chair. "Okay then. Why are you here?"

"Are you going to tell them about the Luna?" inquired Dane.

Alexavier nodded at him. "For my plan to work, I need to tell them."

Dane's eyes sparkled with delight as his hands clapped together in celebration. "Finally!"

Alexavier rolled his eyes at his brother's excitement. "Calm down. Let's go. "

The Alpha and Beta walked towards the open field, the sun warming their skin. As they stepped up to the podium, the members hushed in anticipation.

"Good evening everyone, I know you all are wondering why we are all gathered here today. Well, I have some good news. I found my mate," announced Alexavier.

The members shouted and hollered; the sound filling the air with excitement. While the men whistled, the women's hushed voices rose with questions as their eyes searched the area.

"I can see many of you curiously looking around. My mate is not here with us because she is a human."

Alexavier's mom was beaming from ear to ear while his dad sported a proud smile.

There were gasps from a few of the older women in the pack. The younger men spoke in hushed tones, questioning how an Alpha wolf could be mated to a human.

"The Alpha must have rejected his mate," whispered someone in the crowd.

Alexavier's expression grew stormy and his eyes darkened in response to those words. His deep, menacing growl caused an eerie silence to spread through the crowd.

The members lowered their heads in a sign of submission. They knew it would be unwise to reject the Moon Goddess's blessing.

Annie uttered a whimper under the hard stare her Alpha gave her. She kept her neck lowered in submission.

"I will not be rejecting my mate. The reason I am telling you all of this is so I can assign some of you to aid her while the event is going on. My mate's name is Tasha Williams. She just moved here to work in my company as a designer—" said Alexavier. His face was emotionless, but he was boiling on the inside after Annie's outburst.

"—Who wants to work with their Luna during the event week? I am really asking those who won't be participating in the event," he said. His eyes searched the group.

Alexavier knew he wouldn't have difficulty convincing ten pack members to work during the yearly sports event.

Werewolves were creatures that were loyal to their pack and protecting their leaders. Looking around at the group, he noticed at least forty hands raised. Some of which were people that normally took part in the event.

He handpicked twenty people from the group of forty. He avoided selecting people who usually took part in the event.

When the meeting concluded, Alexavier returned to his office to finish all the other work that was on his plate. He still needed to work out the best way to inform Tasha that she won't be going to another company.

Tasha couldn't wrap her head around the dream she had that night. All she knew was that it was another dream that left her wet and frustrated. Now that she knew Alexavier wasn't married, she couldn't help but fantasize about his naked body against hers.

She savored the feeling of being able to relax and take it easy on Sunday. The only thing she had on her agenda was to stop by the supermarket to buy groceries and a puppy from the pet store.

A tired breath left her lips as she exited the store with her groceries two hours later. She relaxed in her car seat, listening to her favorite song as she drove to the pet store.

Tasha's eyes widened with joy upon seeing the playful puppies, their yelps and yaps filling the air. She couldn't help but smile as she watched the white husky jumping up and down on the fence, trying to get her attention.

That evening, after spending three hours on the road, she cooked stir-fried chicken for dinner.

Her joyful laughter filled the living room as she played with her white fur, blue-eyed husky, Zeus.

Monday came faster than she would have liked. She pulled up to work and tried to get a parking spot close to the building entrance.

As Tasha approached the entrance, Derek hurriedly opened the door for her. She studied him with a skeptical expression, trying to make sense of his peculiar behavior.

His eyes crinkled as he beamed a toothy grin in her direction. "Good morning, Miss Williams."

"Good morning, Derek. Thank you, but you didn't have to open the door for me." She flashed him a grateful smile. Then made her way over to the elevator. She stepped into the waiting elevator and clicked the button for her floor. Derek is acting weird today, she thought, or maybe I'm reading too much into his odd behavior.

It was a long day for Tasha. She felt both drained and baffled. Derek wasn't the only one acting strangely towards her. A lot of the other workers in the building were too.

Some of her department members began calling her boss. A few people even called her, "Luna." When she tried to ask why they were calling her that, they would mumble a hasty excuse before scurrying away.

CHAPTER 15

Wednesday had rolled around and Tasha hadn't caught sight of Alexavier. She knew he had returned to work from his trip. She wanted to know if he had any involvement in how her co-workers were acting. Her annoyance was escalating because of their strange behavior. She was at her wit's end when Mac began to act coldly towards her because of the other employees' behavior. And It appeared Mr. Blu was doing his best to evade her like the plague.

Everyone was preparing to leave for the companies they were scheduled to go to by the end of the week. Yet Tasha still hadn't been emailed the details of the company she was assigned to. The thought of having done something wrong had her in a panic. Maybe Mr. Blu didn't trust me enough to assign me to another corporation.

If it had been any other time, Dane would have howled with laughter at his brother's cowardice. But for now, he had to make sure he didn't cross paths with Tasha. Because he wasn't allowed to give her any information. "Putting your poor brother in your mess," he mumbled to himself. He wanted to avoid having to deceive his Luna.

Dane noticed that the pack members' attitude towards Tasha was leaving her frustrated. The members blundered out of respect for their future Luna. Even though he noticed her distress, he was forbidden from telling her anything. His brother acted as if revealing it would send her running. But Dane had a feeling that she wasn't the kind of person to do that.

Too focused on his own thoughts, Dane didn't see Tasha barreling towards him until it was too late to flee. He would have slapped himself in the face for not sensing her presence. But he was preoccupied, desperately trying to find a way to slip away before she started interrogating him.

"Dane, I don't care if you fire me. I will not hesitate to break your nose if you so much as run without answering me," Tasha whispered through clenched teeth. Her eyes blazed with barely suppressed rage.

Dane could tell from the look in her eyes that she'd had enough of them avoiding her. He could sense the gravity of her words, and knew she would not back down from her threat. His heart raced as he met his Luna's gaze, feeling a mixture of awe and fear. His wolf cringed at her intense gaze, showing submission to her authority.

"What can I help you with, Miss Williams?" he asked. He was trying to keep his face neutral while his heart raced with panic.

"Don't you Miss Williams me, because we both know you have never called me that," she replied. "Where is your brother?" Her eyes narrowed into slits as she waited for his reply.

Dane could have lied, but then it wouldn't be fun for him. He rubbed his chin in contemplation. "I'm sure he's in his office right as we speak."

"Thank you, Dane." She flashed a smile at him before heading towards the elevator.

Tasha stormed out of the elevator as soon as the doors opened. She dashed past Miss White, who was trying to stop her. She refused to allow Alexavier time to come up with an excuse to not see her.

Knocking was the last thing on her mind as she approached his office door. With barely contained rage, she marched into his office. She stopped short at the sight of an older lady talking to him.

Alexavier had felt how angry his mate was at him. But he still hadn't figured out how to tell her his plans for her. He had smelled her scent before she had stormed into his office. The conversation with his mother came to a stop.

His wolf yipped, its tail wagging with happiness at the sight of his mate. Alexavier sighed and pinched the bridge of his nose. His mate had chosen the wrong time to make her grand entrance.

Itana turned in her chair at the sound of the office door being thrown open. She couldn't believe someone would have the nerve to enter her son's office without a warning.

Imagine her shock when noticed the five feet five inches woman standing at the entrance. The fire in Tasha's eyes had Itana feeling sorry for her son. But it was none of her business. She had warned him that avoiding his mate wouldn't solve the problem. Placing her purse on the desk, she got up from the chair and approached Tasha.

"Hi, I'm Itana Blu. The mother of the man you want to kill. You, my dear, can call me Itana," she said. She enveloped the smaller woman in a warm embrace.

Tasha stood frozen with her eyes wide with shock. She cleared her throat as she stepped back when Itana finally released her. "U h... Um... My name is Tasha Williams. I'm the new product designer. As for your son, I only want to punch him in the face for avoiding me, ma'am." Her eyes connected with the man in question after her honest reply. Her eyes shot up at the sound of Itana's laughter.

Tasha had to admit, Alexavier's mother was a beauty. Her hour-glass figure and dark brown skin. The amber-colored eyes that her sons and daughter inherited. Not to mention her height, she was at least five inches taller than Tasha. Her afro hair was like an elegant crown around her oval-shaped face. Which made her look younger than her actual age.

Itana smiled at her soon to be daughter-in-law's honesty. "Well, even if you decide to send him to the hospital, I'm cheering for you. It's nice to finally meet the woman that has my son acting like a teenage boy with a crush. Unfortunately, I must get going now."

"Nice meeting you too, Itana, even though I wish it was under different circumstances," Tasha replied. She returned her deadly glare to the man, staring at his mother with a shocked expression.

Itana hugged Tasha once more before waving to her son. She left the office with a huge smile on her face. She began to plan out in her mind the items she would get for her future grandbabies; the possibilities seeming endless.

Alexavier released a long, resigned sigh when he realized he was about to get an earful from his mate.

Tasha closed the door and made her way over to one of the chairs in front of his desk. "So, are you going to tell me where I'll be going to work while you're gone? Or do you expect me to figure it out by myself, seeing as I'm some type of boss around here now?" Every word laced with the frustration she felt.

Alexavier could tell that his mate's patience had run out. Damn, my mate is sexy when she's angry. His wolf expressed his agreement with a growl.

"Well Miss Williams, it's very unprofessional of you to just storm in here like you own the place. Not to mention I was busy when you did. However, to answer your question. You will be staying here with a few others while most of the workers will be at other companies. I cannot have my designer working at another company because of what happened recently. As for you being called a boss, it's due to you being in charge of everyone while I'm gone," he replied. He tried his best to keep his facial expression neutral. Though his stomach was in knots, waiting for her reaction.

She stood from her seat. Her face voided of any expression as her eyes locked with his. "I hope this has nothing to do with what happened on Saturday. But I understand why you wouldn't want your designer at another company," stated Tasha. Before he could dismiss her, she turned and exited his office.

"Well, she sure behaves like a boss," mumbled Alexavier. His wolf growled, loving his mate's fierce behavior.

He let out a long, exasperated sigh as he returned to his paperwork. "At least that's over with, and she didn't follow through with her threat."

Tasha was filled with joy as she arrived home, knowing Zeus was waiting for her. She wanted to cradle her puppy in her arms, and block out any thought of Alexavier. Her stomach was a knot of nerves and anticipation as she prepared to take charge the following week.

After dinner and a warm shower, she cuddled up next to Zeus in bed. Her heart was pounding as if she was about to witness something big and life-changing. I'll cross that bridge when I get there. She thought, just before sleep took over.

Chapter 16

Everyone was in a frenzy on Friday, doing all they could to make sure everything was ready for their departure.

After work, Tasha went for a jog, needing to collect her thoughts.

Too distracted by her thoughts of being in charge for the upcoming week. She was oblivious to the sight of twenty wolves surrounding her in the forest.

The wolves let out a warning bark, the sound cruel and unfriendly. Some of them had eyes that were completely black and saliva was dripping from their jaws. While others had regular color eyes but looked just as unfriendly.

Tasha took a slow step back, the tension in the air tangible as she tried to think of a way out of the situation. How the hell did I not notice I entered the woods?

Alexavier felt a wave of fear wash over him. But he was in a safe place and nothing was threatening him. The fear he experienced was not severe enough to be associated with his pack members. His thoughts immediately flashed to his mate being in danger. He knew mates could feel each other's emotions and pain. But there was no teaching about mates being able to feel each other's emotions before being marked.

His worry increased as he heard the pitiful whine of his wolf. He didn't even hesitate as he reached for his cellphone to call his mate. She answered after the first ring. But what he heard in the background had him sprinting out of his office, as if he could feel the devil's breath on his neck.

Alexavier's beast snarled at the news that rogues had approached his mate. It was no surprise that the wolves who no longer followed pack laws attacked humans. However, this was no regular human. Tasha was his mate, and he needed to rescue her before they hurt her. It didn't help that she was in neutral territory. A place where rogues roamed freely unless they attacked a pack.

He ordered fifteen of his warriors to meet him at the border. He didn't know how many rogues he was up against. But he knew it was best to get some of his well-trained warriors.

He warned them that their Luna's life was in danger as he changed into his wolf. The cracking of his bones as they reshape was nothing compared to what he had planned for the rogues if his woman was hurt. He headed in the direction that he could sense his mate.

Tasha cursed at Alexavier's awful timing, but with a reluctant sigh, she answered the call. She kept her eyes trained on the twenty wolves surrounding her, their growls growing louder when she answered her phone. At that moment, she wished she had gone to the gym in her apartment complex instead of going for a jog.

The only thing she could hear was the rush of his movements, so she ended the call in haste. It was the worst time for her to be butt dialed by her boss. I need to focus on getting away from these rabid-looking wolves. Spotting an opening on her left side, she pivoted and made a mad dash towards her only way out.

The suddenness of her escape must have taken them off guard. It took a few moments before she could hear them running after her.

She slowed her pace, then reached down to pick up the thick, broken branch that was lying on the forest ground. She slid to a stop and turned to swing at the nearest wolf. Imagine her shock when the wolf she hit collided with another.

The two wolves tumbled to the ground, their yelps echoing through the forest and whimpered in despair.

Not dwelling on her newfound strength, she continued running for her life.

Tasha was running out of energy, but the rabid wolves were still hot on her heels. She sensed a wolf was about to pounce, and quickly ducked. Just as she did that, she felt the breeze from the wolf's leap. Without hesitation, she twisted her body slightly and swung the branch upwards. The branch slammed against the wolf's stomach, and she smirked in triumph. Her smirk was short-lived, however, when she saw the others surrounding her once again. Groaning in annoyance, she glared at them.

Her heart felt as if it had stopped at the sound of bones cracking. Right in front of her, the thing she'd only ever seen in her dreams was happening in reality. She would have fainted if her life wasn't at stake. Now standing four feet away from her was a naked rough-looking man. She could tell he hadn't bathed in days, if not weeks, from the patches of dirt that coated his body.

"You know, for a small human woman, you're pretty strong. You knocked out one of my men. The other has a few broken ribs, and the third is still whimpering like a baby. I bet you're wondering if you're dreaming and why we are chasing you?" The man spoke. He licked his dry lips as he stared at the woman his mate ordered them to capture.

Tasha arched a brow at the man. He cannot be serious right now. She wanted nothing more than her situation to be a dream. She didn't care to listen to why they chose her for their meal choice.

Her eyes roamed the area for an escape. "Normally I'd welcome the information, but today I'm not that curious to stick around. Plus, I have somewhere to be and it definitely isn't in the stomach of you wolves," she replied. She took a step back as she prepared to attack.

"Not so fast. I'm sure you wanna stick around to see who joins the party next," he said with a growl. His eyes danced with amusement. He had sniffed out the Blue Moon Pack's Alpha and warriors approaching. His fellow rogue mates tensed in response to the overwhelming presence of power.

Tasha was about to tell him to go to hell, but then she heard a ground-shaking growl. A growl that sent a familiar shiver through her. Her eyes darted in the direction of the growl for the newcomer. The fact that her body responded like that to the growl of a wolf was something she refused to acknowledge at that moment.

The sight of her wolf bursting through the trees was a welcome sight to her. It had brought along fifteen other wolves of different colors. Her body relaxed as she stared into his golden eyes. Her eyes flickered over to the man whose smirk seemed to have widened at her wolf's presence. She tilted her head to the side in confusion, her brows furrowed.

Her wolf walked over to her while his pack mates surrounded the crazy-looking wolves. She wasn't able to stop herself from running her fingers through his fur. The rumble that followed made her smile. She felt safe with him there. The man's threatening growl reverberated through the air, interrupting their moment.

"Ahhh... Mr. Big bad Alpha has finally joined us. I wonder why? Did you come to rescue a dismal in distress? Or did you come to rescue your precious human?" asked the man. He placed a hand on his chin in thought. "I found it weird when I smelt an Alpha scent on a human." He didn't want the Alpha to know he was there to kidnap the woman.

Tasha was perplexed as she watched the man speaking to the wolf, as if expecting an answer. Her mind refused to process that her wolf was just like the wolves that chased her. Until what he said finally clicked. "What do you mean by his scent? I haven't seen this wolf since last Friday." She stared at the man, wondering if his nose was working right.

"Oh! She doesn't know, and to think she would put two and two together. Seeing as I just transformed from wolf to man in front of her," he said, not answering her question.

CHAPTER 17

Alexavier growled, hearing enough from the rogue. He ordered his wolves to attack. Shielding Tasha with his large body, he cautiously observed the leader of the rogue group. The man's scent was kind of familiar to him. But he couldn't place where he'd smelt the scent before.

Alexavier bared his teeth and growled when he sensed a rogue drawing near. He turned to face the wolf while still keeping his mate behind him. The smaller rogue lunged itself at Alexavier, who stood on his hind legs to meet it.

Their jaws clashed and the smaller wolf tried to bite the Alpha's neck.

Alexavier swiped his claws over the small wolf's fur. The wolf whimpered and tried to distance itself. A snarl left Alexavier before he pounced onto the smaller wolf and sank his teeth into its neck — killing it.

The leader of the group didn't like that the Alpha had his pack warriors attacking his followers. He changed back to his wolf and circled the Alpha, trying to get to the human. I'll capture her and bring her back to my mate, even if it's the last thing I do.

Alexavier watched the leader of the rogues movement keenly. Blood dripped from his mouth as he snarled his warning. As the rogue charged forward, Alexavier followed suit, his fangs biting into the rogue's neck.

The rogue used his front two paws to push the Alpha off.

The alpha wolf bared his teeth, the sound of a growl rumbling from his chest as he leapt at the rogue. The two wolves collided in a flurry of fur, claws, and teeth.

Alexavier was able to sink his canines into the other wolf's neck once again. He shook his head while clamping down on the whimpering wolf's neck. When he felt the rogue leader's body go limp, he reluctantly released him.

Tasha was so entranced by the way her wolf fought she failed to notice the wolf steadily moving towards her. A snarl filled the air, and she turned around only for the wolf to jump on top of her. A scream rose from her throat at the impact. Despite the pain, she battled the wolf in an effort to keep it from biting her. As a last resort, she used her legs to kick the wolf off her.

Alexavier's heart plummeted when he heard his mate cry out. He turned with a savage snarl, a fierce growl rumbling in his throat as he prepared to protect his mate. He watched as the rogue attempted to regain his footing after the kick.

Alexavier's low, menacing growl reverberated through the forest. His fur bristled as he stalked toward the rogue. His claws dug into the dirt as he prepared to pounce. However, his mate blocked his path, preventing him from finishing off the rogue. His lips curled back as he released a warning growl.

Tasha arched an eyebrow at her wolf before smacking it with a branch she had found. "Back away from this one. He's mine! You had your fun with the filthy leader. I think I deserve this one. After all, I'm the one that was being chased," said Tasha.

Alexavier let out a fierce growl, then took a few steps back from the rogue. He turned to scan the area, checking on his pack warriors. When he saw everyone was doing fine on their own, he turned back to his mate.

The rogue wolf bared its teeth and let out a menacing growl as Tasha stepped closer. She smirked, knowing it wouldn't dare attack with her wolf nearby. She swung the branch with all her might onto the wolf's head. Her eyes closed tight in repulsion at the sickening crack of the impact. The wolf fell a few feet away from where it had been, with blood gushing from his head.

Alexavier's eyes widened in shock at his mate's strength. He was not expecting her to do so much damage with a branch. His chest swelled with pride as he watched his mate willingly protect herself.

Tasha dropped the branch in her hand and turned towards her wolf. Her eyes burned with fury and her words were laced with venom. "Do you want to shift now or continue acting like you're not one of them?"

Alexavier growled at her tone. Even though she was his mate, he did not appreciate being disrespected. "Gamma Shane, you and the others can head back to the house. Tell the omegas to come clean up this mess," he ordered through the mind-link.

His eyes then returned to his fuming mate to check if she had any severe injuries. His shoulders relaxed when he noticed she had not been badly injured. Just a few bumps and scrapes. He shifted, not caring that she would see his naked body. After all, he was hers if she accepted him.

"Oh, dear God! You couldn't go behind a tree to change? Where are your clothes?" She exclaimed at the sight of his naked body.

He smirked at her shyness. "What you didn't think about that when you not so nicely asked me to shift? Plus, you shouldn't be shy about this. You've seen me like this and in naughtier ways in your dreams many times." His eyes glowed with amusement as he playfully teased his mate, loving her innocence.

Tasha would have punched him for his cocky words if she wasn't feeling the pain of dropping on her back. She tried not to let her eyes travel past his waist and rolled her eyes at his teasing.

"You know, you're handling all this pretty well. Are you sure you didn't already know werewolves existed before being chased by those rogues?" He rubbed his chin as he studied his little mate.

"Well, after meeting you when I've been dreaming about you since I was sixteen, kind of helped. It's not everyday someone meets someone they've only seen in their dreams. Let's not forget I've seen you shifting from man to wolf in those same dreams. This whole situation just proves that my dreams meant more than just a simple dream. It's a little shocking to see it in reality, but fainting wasn't on my to do list while trying to stay alive." She stared at her boss's face as she finished her sentence.

Alexavier's heart felt light after hearing his mate's thoughts about the situation. Maybe she won't reject him after all. He felt the corners of his lips tugging up in a smirk as the thought occurred to him. "I'm guessing it's safe to say you've dreamt of me naked, then. Because you haven't closed the distance between us.

Even though I know you're itching to punch me. Are you afraid you would follow through with your erotic thoughts?"

Tasha muttered curses under her breath. She refused to meet his eyes, her gaze locked instead on the leaves of the trees. She would never admit that what he said was the truth. If her dreams were anything to go by, they shared a connection that would have her behaving like a dog in heat.

He laughed at her colorful choice of words. "I'm going to shift into my wolf and you're going to climb onto my back." He shifted before she could disagree with his command. He laid flat on the ground, waiting for her to climb on.

The possibility of riding on the back of her wolf sent a thrill down her spine, so she accepted the offer without hesitation. She felt the warmth of his fur as she climbed onto his back, and her eyes lit up with excitement.

When Alexavier felt her tightly gripping his fur, he took off in the direction of the pack-house. His mate's presence in his territory made him feel alive with joy. The territory that would also be hers once she accepted him. They zoomed in and out of trees. He leapt over fallen logs as he and his wolf enjoyed the sound of their mate's laughter.

Tasha marveled at the houses that varied in size as they made their way further into the forest. Every house was adorned with intricate, unique architecture. She thought it would be full of trees, but that wasn't the case. Instead, there were wide lands of green grass with beautiful flowers in different areas.

As she passed, she caught a glimpse of the children playing on the swings in the park. But the thing that took her breath away was the house, no mansion — her wolf stopped in front. The bright lights of the house shone brightly as the sky grew darker.

She had to admit her boss had good taste for having such a wonderful house built. However, before she could tell him that. She noticed at least a hundred people surrounding them.

Some of them smiled warmly at her, while others were studying her intently. She recognized some of them from work. So she smiled at them, wondering why they were all staring at her. She felt his presence next to her and turned to ask him her question. But before she could get a word out, he started talking.

Chapter 18

Dianna stood in her home, her screams echoing off the walls of the warehouse. Her soul felt as if someone had ripped it in half. Her need for revenge had cost her the life of her mate. She wept, the tears of anguish streaming down her face, accompanied by a soft whimper of sorrow. It was too much for her; she didn't expect to lose him.

The rogues that followed Dianna and her mate echoed their sorrow through the night air with their haunting howls. The despair that filled the room when Dianna cried told them she had lost half of her soul. Their ice cold leader had lost the only person who could keep her anger in check.

It hit them like a ton of bricks that they had not only lost their best warrior, but a great number of their best fighters as well. The group kept a close eye on their leader, their faces soft with sympathy as they tried to offer her a sense of comfort from afar. No one dared to approach the female in mourning. They all feared she would snap and kill them all.

After losing their mate, a werewolf became emotionally and mentally unstable. Those that weren't strong enough to withstand the death of their mate died from grief or self harm. It didn't matter if they had children, they would rather die than live without their soulmate.

Gloria entered the makeshift office that her daughter-in-law occupied. Her own tears fell as she watched how broken the powerful female looked after losing her mate. She felt her own heart crumble, her one and only child taken from her too soon.

The older woman quietly wept on the couch near her daughter-in-law. She was wary of Dianna's plan from the start, sensing it would only bring trouble. But no matter how much she wanted to, she couldn't blame Dianna for the result. She knew that a woman like her daughter-in-law was prideful and would seek retribution at some point.

"You need to end this before you lose your life. My son risked his life for you, knowing he was no match for an Alpha. You need to put the past behind you, Dianna," whispered Gloria.

Dianna's eyes became as cold as a winter's night. Her eyes were burning with barely contained rage as her lips curled into a snarl. Her wolf's angry growls echoed through her mind, desperate for the taste of blood. She turned away from her mother-in-law and stormed out of the warehouse that they were temporarily calling home.

As her tears slowly evaporated, Dianna's heart was consumed with a dark, unquenchable thirst for revenge. She ventured through the forest, feeling the dried leaves beneath her feet as she planned her next move. Her legs gave way, a mile away from Alexavier's territory.

She felt a heavy weight of guilt settling in her chest as she realized she had lost her mate and followers because of her revengeful
desires. All I requested was for them to capture Alexavier's mate. I
never ask them to fight in order to kidnap the woman.

"Why?!" she screamed into the forest. Birds took to the sky and
other small creatures ran from the sound of the predator.

She felt a deep, burning rage towards the man who had cruelly
evicted her from her home. A rage so strong that she jumped at the
chance to capture Alexavier's mate the minute she heard about
her.

As she remained seated on the forest ground, her mind flashback
to three years ago. The years when she was still living with her
family and pack friends. Even though she was just a pack warrior's
daughter, she'd always hoped to be Alexavier's mate. When they'd
turned sixteen, she realized they weren't mates. She spent years
trying to persuade him to choose her as his Luna, but he refused
to.

One night, Dianna took a risk and snuck into Alexavier's room,
and tried to mark him. Even though she had been careful, her plan
was unsuccessful.

He had smelled her before she even reached his neck. He rose
from his bed and shoved her into the wall across the room.

The force he used had her slumped against the wall. She experienced a roller coaster of emotions that night, starting with a sense
of hope and ending in darkness and despair.

"Bring her to the dungeon. I will deal with her in the morning,"
ordered Alexavier.

The two guards that had rushed to the Alpha's quarters bowed before dragging her away. Alexavier's cold, piercing eyes met hers before he turned away.

Dianna knew well that it was unacceptable to mark another without their permission. But in her desperation to make him hers, she had no regard for the consequences. All she wanted was him, and she was sick of being rejected by him every time. What she didn't expect was for him to banish her the next day.

"Listen up everyone! I know you all want a chance to talk to Tasha. But she was nearly killed by rogues earlier and requires her injuries to be tended to—" said Alexavier.

The reactions from the crowd were immediate; a gasp of disbelief, followed by a wave of angry growls. Their eyes widened as they scanned their future Luna's body and noticed the wounds on her exposed skin.

"—Some warriors and I took care of those rogues, of course. But right now I need to explain things to her and tend to her injuries so that when you talk to her, she's comfortable," said Alexavier. He knew how anxious the members were ever since they learned about their new luna. "That's it for now."

Tasha turned to face Alexavier when she felt the brush of his hand against her arm. He motioned with his head for her to follow him. They both entered the pack-house.

She admired how beautiful the inside was. Everything was pristine and grand, from the white velvet furniture to the intricately painted ceiling. They had to climb the majestic, winding stairway that was in the middle of the living room.

When Alexavier stepped onto the second floor, he turned right, and her footsteps echoed behind him. Her eyes wandered around the hall as they walked. Photos of different wolves and people lined the walls.

Alexavier stopped at his office's double doors and waited for Tasha, who had fallen behind.

Tasha watched as he walked with confidence toward his desk. She smiled at his behavior and walked towards the chair that was in front of his desk. She sat with her hands folded across her chest and a brow raised.

Alexavier opened the desk drawer slowly, pulling out the first aid kit with a muffled clank. He walked around his desk and knelt in front of a surprised Tasha. His eyes roamed her form, searching for the visible cuts she had gotten while running from the rogues.

He opened the kit and pulled out all the things he needed to take care of her. "I was going to wait until we went on our first date to tell you about us. But seeing as your life is in danger, it's only right for me to tell you now," he said with a grimed look. His eyes remained focused on her arm that he was dressing.

Her eyes grew wide at the mention of a date and her heart raced at the prospect of going on one with him. She tried to keep her cool and gestured for him to continue with the hand he wasn't holding. She hissed in pain as his hand brushed over a deep cut on her right knee.

Alexavier's eyes widened as they met hers, his worries plain on his face. "I'm sorry." He tenderly blew on her knee, the gentle breeze soothing some of her pain.

Her lips quirked up into a soft smile and she lightly rested her hand on his. "I'm okay. It doesn't hurt that bad. You can continue talking. I really want to know why I was being chased."

Alexavier slowly inhaled, trying to calm the nerves that were bubbling up inside of him before he told her. "Well, the rogues that you encountered today were after you because they somehow learned that you're my mate. No one outside of my pack was to know this information. Which means someone in my pack has been running their mouth. When I find the culprit, they're going to regret being born." His voice had a sharp, steel edge.

"How did being friends with you cause such rabid animals to come after me? And what are rogues, exactly?" Asked Tasha. She studied his face, searching for answers, while his hands worked to finish bandaging her knee with a gentle touch.

Alexavier sighed as he placed the items back into the kit. His eyes met hers, and he could feel the intensity of her gaze as he stayed kneeling in front of her.

His wolf basked in the warmth of his mate's gaze. "No Tasha, a mate in the werewolves' world does not mean friends. It means soulmate or your destined half that werewolves are blessed to have. But it's easier to just say mate."

He paused as he studied her features. His eyes closed when he recalled how the wolf had jumped on his mate. "Rogues are wolves who left their pack willingly or were kicked out by their Alpha. Some scum to their wolves and are more wolf than human. Those wolves have completely black eyes. Then there are those who still have their humanity but kill without a reason."

"But I'm not a werewolf, so how can I be your mate?" She was happy to know he belonged to her. Still, she feared it might be a mistake.

"There are a few wolves that have been blessed with human mates. We don't get to choose. Although it's the first time an alpha's mate is human. The jolt of electricity that surged through us when we met and the constant tingles when we touch are proof we are mates," answered Alexavier. He studied her intently, watching her face to capture every flicker of emotion. He had sensed her fear, and he wanted to remove them.

Tasha nodded in understanding. Her gaze locked with his as a sudden thought emerged in her mind. "So, is that why I've been seeing you in my dreams for so long?"

"Yes, I believe that's the reason. I think it's how the Moon Goddess helped to guide you to me. I've been asking other werewolves with human mates about it. So far, you are the only one to dream about your mate," answered Alexavier.

He picked up the kit from the floor and made his way to his chair behind his desk. He took a seat before he continued talking, "we will continue this mate talk when I take you out to breakfast tomorrow. Right now, I need to figure out how to draw out whoever is trying to use the rogues to kill you and why."

"Well, then I'll leave you to it." As she got up to leave the office, an aching sensation in her back caused her to freeze. Stupid rabid wolves, she growled in her mind. She bit down hard on her lip to muffle the groan that threatened to escape, aware of his eyes on her. When the pain subsided, she shifted her gaze to meet his, and the realization that he had asked her out settled in. "As in a date?"

Alexavier's eyes crinkled with his smile as he nodded at her. He'd watched her make a feeble attempt to suppress her anguish, and he could feel his anger rising. He knew that if he checked her body for other bruises, it would displease her. And she would refuse to admit that she was in pain even if he asked the pack doctor for help.

"Um...Who will be taking me home?" she whispered. She ginger-ly made her way to the door, careful not to jostle her bruised back. Alexavier's next sentence had her freezing mid-step...

CHAPTER 19

"You're spending the night here."

Tasha couldn't believe the words that he'd said to her. How can he just expect me to spend the night surrounded by a pack of unknown wolves? She had a home and a dog she needed to get back to. His nonchalant attitude as he spoke those words made her blood boil. The bruise on her back was momentarily forgotten as she spun to face him, her rage visible—before she marched out of his office.

The fuming Luna's presence was so powerful that all the pack members instinctively moved aside.

A pack of werewolves is afraid of little old me. She would have laughed at their actions at any other time. But she was busy planning how to castrate Alexavier Blu. A plan she would happily execute if she wasn't surrounded by his pack.

"How dare he try to order me to stay?" she mumbled to herself. "I was doing fine when the rogues attacked me. I didn't need his protection. Mate or not, I will not put up with him telling me what to do."

Her mumbles trailed off as her gaze fell upon the sight of a car garage in the distance. She curled her lips into a sinister smirk as she thought about her next move. When she entered the garage, a feeling of excitement coursed through her as her eyes fell upon just what she was looking for. Grabbing the keys off the key hook, she unlocked Alexavier's Porsche.

Her smile stretched from ear to ear as the engine roared to life. She drove out of the garage and was about to take the only road path when she noticed Dane heading towards the house. It wasn't Dane that caught her eyes but, more so, the little fur-ball that was licking at his cheek. She would have laughed, but the sight of her new pup being there caught her off guard. Tasha got out of the car and slammed the door shut.

Dane jumped at the sound of a car door slamming. He cringed, wondering who was so thoughtless. But at the sight of Tasha coming from said car, he wished it was someone else. He felt a lump in his throat as he watched her lips curl up into a sinister smirk. The little husky felt more like a heavy burden he was not prepared to bear.

"How the hell did you get into my apartment and who told you to take my dog?" Asked Tasha. Her gaze was intense, her eyes burning with rage.

Gulping loudly, he answered, "I got the keys from Mr. Henry and it's all Alexavier's doing." He wanted to hide. He'd never seen her so angry, and it scared him. His wolf whimpered in his mind, feeling the power of their Luna.

"He did what!" Exclaimed Tasha.

Her puppy yelped in response to its owner's booming voice.

All eyes outside were drawn to the future Luna as her voice reached a fever pitch, wondering who was on the receiving end of her wrath. The older pack members could see that the Luna was no regular human. Her voice held authority and she could make even the strongest wolf cower.

Tasha took Zeus from Dane, the soft fur of his body brushing against her hands. Her shoulder bumped into Dane as she headed back to Alexavier's office. With every step she took up the stairs, her mind formulated ideas on how to end the aggravating wolf.

Alexavier could feel the anger radiating from his mate before he even laid eyes on her. When his mate stormed into his office that night, he knew he was in for an explosive confrontation. He braced himself for her outburst.

"How dare you tell your people to enter my home without my permission?! That's an invasion of my fucking privacy, Mr. Blu. I was willing to brush aside you trying to order me to spend the night at your place. But you sending Dane into my home shows how little you respect my fucking feelings. If this is how you wolves treat your mate, you can kiss me giving you a chance goodbye," she said with ice dripping behind each word.

Even though her heart knew he was trying to protect her, she was furious at him.

Alexavier let out a growl in response to her disrespectful tone. His wolf couldn't tolerate being disrespected, and he was frustrated that his mate refused his protection.

Alexavier rose from his chair, his movements slow and deliberate as he strode towards his mate. His eyes glowed a molten gold. "I'll let your disrespect slide once more because you're new to our world."

He stared into her raging eyes as he continued talking, loving the challenge. "First and foremost, you are my equal, and I do care about your feelings and opinions. However, we wolves, or should I say we alphas, take protecting our mate seriously. You won't feel comfortable sleeping in your own home after what you went through earlier. I would rather have you here where you'll feel safe knowing I'm around to protect you. Even if you hate me now, you'll get over it. The moment you entered my life, you became my world. My wolf and I live to protect and take care of your needs. All your needs."

Alexavier stopped a foot away from Tasha, the air between them thick with tension. Her little puppy started growling at him. A warning that it wasn't pleased with how close danger was to its human.

Alexavier bared his teeth at the dog before bending down to whisper next to his mate's ear. "Now you can follow me to your room for the night or I can carry you there, kicking and screaming. You look tired. And Love, believe that I would enjoy doing the latter."

Tasha's breath was caught in her throat as she felt his gentle breath against her ear. Her traitorous heart fluttered when he offered to carry her to her room.

Alexavier stepped back with a teasing smirk covering his lip, loving her reaction. His smirk quickly turned to shock when he felt the sharp little teeth of the husky grazing his skin. He raised a brow at Tasha, who was now sporting a smirk of her own.

Tasha scratched behind Zeus's ear, happy that he was willing to protect her from the giant in front of her. The rage she had felt before had melted away after his explanation, and she blamed it on being his mate.

She looked over her shoulder at her mate as she was exiting his office. "Pull a stunt like that again, and I'll make sure Zeus bites you where it will hurt the most."

Alexavier gave her a subtle nod, but his eyes sparkled with amusement. He walked out of his office with them and shut the door behind him.

They took the stairs to the fourth floor, which only had three bedrooms on it. The biggest room being the Alpha and Luna's room.

Tasha huffed out a breath of exhaustion as they reached the fourth floor. She felt the pain in her back intensify as she continued to carry Zeus. As she bent to place the little husky on the floor, a low, pained groan escaped her lips.

Alexavier rushed to her side. His furrowed brow and down turned lips showed his concern. "Are you okay? Where does it hurt? I'll go get the doctor." His hand rested gently on her shoulder as he looked for any other signs of injury.

She released a sigh as the pain eased from his touch. Her eyes locked with his, and she could sense his worry in the intensity of his gaze. "I'm fine. It's just a little back pain from the fall. Something that a hot shower and rest will fix."

He studied his mate's face. She seemed to be in less pain while his hand remained on her shoulder. "Stay here. I'll go get a shirt from my closet for you to wear to bed."

Tasha tried to smile at him when he removed his hand, but the pain was too much. A soft whimper fell from her lips as she leaned against the wall for support.

Alexavier walked out of one of the rooms with a white shirt and boxers in hand. He gently placed his hand on the small of her back, guiding her across the hall to the room opposite his.

After opening the door for her, he handed her the shirt and boxers before allowing her to enter her room. "Please tell me if the pain gets worse so that I can get the doctor to do a checkup," said Alexavier.

She smiled at him. "Thank you. I'll let you know if the pain gets too uncomfortable."

Alexavier returned her smile. "Have a wonderful shower and rest, mate." He closed her door and went back to his office.

Chapter 20

After a peaceful night's rest, Tasha woke up energized and ready to tackle the day ahead. The pain in her back had vanished, and a broad grin spread across her face. She paused, her cat-like stretching, when she realized Zeus was no longer by her side. She frantically searched the room for him, but when she found no trace, she bolted out of the room.

She paid no attention to her hair, which likely resembled a bird's nest. And that she was wearing only Alexavier's shirt and his boxers. All she could think about was the desperate need to find Zeus in the wolves' den.

Alexavier was astonished as he stood in the kitchen, preparing food for his mate's dog. The little dog's whine awoke him, so he went to check his mate's room. He felt something was amiss when he heard the pup cries, but then he realized the pup was just hungry.

It amazed him that his mate could sleep through all the noise her dog was making. He was certain that half the pack was up early because of said cries.

The moment he gave the dog the cooked meat, the sound of his mate's feet pounding on the kitchen floor filled the room. Her eyes were wide and searching, as if she had lost the most precious thing in the world.

Alexavier's heart warmed at the sight of her, and his face broke out into a smile. Even with a messy bedhead, she radiated beauty. His shirt on her was very appealing to his eyes.

Tasha noticed Alexavier in the kitchen and was about to question him about her dog's disappearance. But she didn't need to because he was already pointing towards her husky eating. She sighed in relief and turned to head back to her room. However, she felt her body being lifted and thrown over someone's shoulder. From the eruption of butterflies in her belly, she knew whose back she was facing. "Um... Alexavier, what are you doing?"

He froze mid-step at the way she said his name. The warmth in her voice as she said his name for the first time sent a thrill through him. He cleared his throat, "do you see what you're wearing around unmated wolves?"

Tasha groaned in fake annoyance. His husky voice sent a shiver down her spine, and her heartbeat quickened. "Well, the way you're carrying me doesn't help the situation." She was trying to be stern, but her words were nothing more than a breathless whisper.

Alexavier growled at a guy passing by and continued up the stairs.

Tasha rolled her eyes at his possessive behavior, but her eyes gleamed with delight at witnessing this side of her mate. She felt him grab her hips, and then she felt the sensation of her body slowly sliding down his body until her feet hit the floor.

She turned away from him, needing some space. The room felt too hot even as she felt a light breeze coming in through the window. Wait, breeze? Her head snapped up, and she was shocked to find herself in his room instead of her own.

"Uh... Why am I in your room?" Her eyes roamed the room. Dark blue walls with a few picture frames. White satin sheets covered his king-size bed. A glass sliding door opened up to a balcony. Of course, his room is enormous.

Alexavier threw her one of his smallest joggers. "Put those on so we can go get breakfast."

Tasha caught the joggers just before it hit her in the face. She glared at him as she got dressed. The joggers were a bit big, but she made it work.

Tasha asked Dane to watch Zeus before she left with Alexavier. They went to IHOP for breakfast and she had to admit, even though he was a possessive jerk sometimes. She enjoyed spending time with him.

He told her more about mates and what role a luna played in the pack. She had to admit that, despite feeling scared, this new world was captivating. And deep down, she was dying to know more about her soulmate.

After picking up Zeus from the pack-house, Alexavier took Tasha home. She spent the rest of the day playing with Zeus, basking in the afternoon's warmth, and daydreaming about her mate.

The pack had only one day left to prepare for the sports event. The excitement was plastered across everyone's faces.

Alexavier was thrilled. He frequently participated in a variety of sports, but soccer was his favorite. His team had won the soccer title, and he remembered all too well the look of disappointment when Dane's team had come second the year before.

On Sunday, Alexavier went to visit his mate. He handed her a thick folder with all the tasks he wanted her and the other twenty workers to complete. He handed her a slip of paper with the security codes she needed to gain access to the building. They spent the rest of the day curled up on the couch, getting to know each other and watching movies.

Tasha learned he liked all shades of blue and that he loved being the alpha. Her mate was a bad boy in high school and popular in college. He preferred staying home than going out whenever he had free time. He enjoyed watching anime when he was younger and he played a lot of games with his brother and best friend Shane.

Alexavier learned that his mate was a tomboy who was fond of the color rose pink. He also learned that she had only one best friend named Jade. His mate and her best friend had trained for a few years in kickboxing. He noticed that his mate spoke little about her parents, but he didn't pressure her about it. His mate loved telling jokes and enjoyed anime as much as him.

When he finally decided to leave, he told Tasha to be careful. And to call him if any emergency arose.

Tasha's stomach was in knots as she thought of Monday, but she was determined to hold her ground. By leaving her with the company, Alexavier showed her he had faith in her capabilities. So she was going to do her best to make him proud. She picked out her outfit for work the next day. Which comprised navy blue formal work pants, a blazer to match, and a white dress shirt.

She called her best friend, who she hadn't spoken to in days. The phone rang a few times before Jade finally answered.

"Hey best friend, how are you?" Jade answered. She was panting heavily, her breath coming out in ragged gasps.

"Hey bestie, I'm good and how are you? Did I interrupt something? You sound like you just ran a marathon?" Tasha asked.

"If you mean, was I getting my pussy worked? Then yes, my dear Tasha, I was running a marathon."

"For the love of God Jade! Too much information you couldn't have just said yes and left it at that."

Jade's laughter was followed by her deep breaths, which reverberated through the phone speaker. "And what would be fun about that? You know, he was just about to flip me on my belly with my butt facing up when you called."

Tasha was so embarrassed that she felt like she wanted to crawl into a hole. But was happy to know her best friend was having fun. "As long as I'm a godmother, you can continue working on those children."

Jade released a hearty chuckle. The guy beside her gave her a questioning look as he heard her bubbly laughter fill the air. Instead of answering him, she answered Tasha, "that will only happen when you start getting some tender loving. Because, girl, you are missing out."

Tasha's lips quirked up in amusement. She shook her head at her best friend's antics, deciding it was best to not answer that. "Goodnight Jade, and please don't break the poor guy. It seems like he didn't get the memo when he decided to approach you."

The speakers filled with a tinkling sound of Jade's laughter. Her best friend knew her too well. "Good night, bestie, and no promises."

While Tasha was still pure as the clouds, her best friend was a whole other story. Despite all that, she never judged her or stopped loving Jade.

Jade was the definition of gorgeous. A woman that loved rocking her natural hair in an afro, if she wasn't wearing a protective style like—box braids or cornrows. She stood no taller than five feet, with a curvy body. Her dark brown eyes matched her melanin skin. In Tasha's eyes, her best friend was flawless.

Closing her eyes, she allowed sleep to pull her in.

Monday morning came sooner than Tasha would have liked. However, she was ready for her first day as a boss. She did her usual morning routine before heading out for work. She arrived at the work building earlier than usual. With the intention of assisting the security in setting everything up.

At eight o'clock on the dot, everyone that was working with her for the week was present.

Tasha stood tall and proud, her chin held high. She distributed copies of her list of tasks to be accomplished by the end of the day to each person.

As the day progressed, Tasha walked around, her hands patting people's shoulders in support as she checked on them. She was unfamiliar with the duties that others had been assigned.

Despite the challenges, she still attempted to lend a hand when they were having difficulty with their tasks.

At approximately five o'clock in the evening, everyone had left or was getting ready to leave. Tasha and Derek started locking up.

With the security system activated, she waved goodbye to Derek and drove out of the parking lot.

The pack members were ready for the events to begin. The first event was track and field. Shane was in charge of the adults that were taking part. Dane was in charge of the teenagers and Alexavier was in charge of the children from three years to twelve.

There were three teams, and each team had thirty participants. Team Alpha was dressed in blue, Team Beta in red, and Team Gamma in purple. With Tasha's addition to the pack, a fourth team would be created and called Team Luna.

For the adult section, Team Alpha was in the lead. In the teens' section, Team Gamma and the children's section Team Beta. The atmosphere was charged with excitement as the cheer of the crowd filled the air. Those who weren't playing in the game were standing on the sidelines, cheering and waving flags for their chosen team.

The last race came to a close at seven-thirty at night. Team Beta took the lead, a wave of excitement rippling through the crowd on day one. While Team Alpha was in second and Team Gamma last.

After dinner, Alexavier called Tasha to find out how her day went. His heart fluttered when he heard her breath on the other end of the phone. "Hello, mate. How was your day?"

Tasha beamed while her hand continued to run through Zeus's fur. "Hi Mr. Blu. Hmm, my day went great. Everyone was nice and helpful. How was your day?"

"I'm happy to hear your day went great. Mine was fun, but it was not the outcome I hoped for." He smiled as he recalled the feeling of pride that radiated from his mate's coworkers when they returned home.

The pack members that had worked with her had told him how nice and kind she was. He could tell that working with their soon-to-be Luna made them happy.

Tasha smiled at the pride in her mate's voice. "What did you do today?" Her voice was playful as she relaxed into her pillow.

"Today was the track and field event. Dane's team won," replied Alexavier with a small pout. "Our team was neck to neck in the older folks' races, but..."

She stifled a yawn as he continued talking. His voice had a calming effect, and it wasn't long before she drifted off to sleep. She hoped the following day would be just as good, if not better.

CHAPTER 21

Tuesday was a battle for Tasha, as she could not get to work on time since Zeus wouldn't let her go. She found his behavior bizarre and was tempted to call in sick. But she was in charge of the company.

It resulted in her calling Dane for help. When he answered his phone, she could hear the anxiety in her voice as she asked, "Hey Dane, can you puppy sit for me today?"

"Hey Tasha, yes sure. I'll come pick him up. Just leave the spare key with Mr. Henry."

"Thanks, Dane. I'll come for him after work."

"No problem. Bye."

"Bye!" Tasha turned towards her whining pup, who had blocked the door. "Dane is coming to get you, so be a good boy for mommy, okay?"

Zeus had looked up at her with a judging expression before huffing in frustration. He stayed at the door whining even after she'd left the apartment.

In her office, the sound of clicking keyboards surrounded Tasha as she worked diligently to finish her day's assignments. The sudden, sharp knock on her office door made her jump, and she felt herself falling out of her chair.

Felicia, a fierce warrior in the pack, heard her future Luna's shriek and flung the office door open. She feared for the worst, but she was surprised to see the Luna on the floor rubbing her bottom.

Instead of helping Tasha off the floor, Felicia started laughing. Tasha gave her an icy death glare that made her instinctively try to muffle it with a cough.

"Um... I'm sorry for startling you. I came by to ask for your help. I knocked on your door a few times, but you did not respond," said a smiling Felicia.

Tasha got up off the floor, dusting off her pants. She leaned back in her chair and studied the young woman's face. "What can I help you with...?" she trailed off, waiting for a name.

"Oh, my bad. My name is Felicia Andrews and I work in the AutoCAD department. We need your help with one of the drawings, Miss Williams."

"I'd be happy to help Miss Andrews. Please call me Tasha." She beamed as she pushed herself out of her chair. She motioned for Felicia to lead the way.

"Yes Luna," replied Felicia.

"I'm guessing you have to address me by my last name or Luna because of pack status?" She quirked a brow at Felicia as they walked side by side.

"Yes, Luna." Felicia smiled at her future Luna. Tasha's calm, patient nature gave the feeling that she would be an excellent Luna.

Tasha gave her a curt nod. She was beginning to recognize the contrast between werewolves and humans. Werewolves had a beauty about them that seemed flawless.

The men had sharp jawlines and were naturally built. Their aura screamed dominance and seemed to be more present the higher up they were in status. She remembered how she felt whenever her eyes connected with the Blu brothers. The feeling of a prey being watched by a predator. They also seemed to age like fine wine. It was hard for her to guess the members' ages just by looking at them. Tallness seemed to be a common trait in all of them, even the women.

All the women seemed to have figures that resembled an hour-glass. The young woman walking beside her was a prime example. She stood at least four inches taller than Tasha. Her dark skin looked flawless and her work outfit was tailored for her body. Her dreadlocks brushed her hips as she walked.

Tasha felt like her blood pressure was about to burst. Two hours it took them, two freaking hours to figure out how to get the missing part of the design back. This was the reason she hated AutoCAD. The software gave her more headaches than she could count. She didn't normally get this irritated at things like this. So she figured something else had to be happening.

She quickly grabbed her phone and dialed Alexavier's number. He answered after four rings, which surprised her because it usually takes only one ring for him to answer.

"Hey Tasha, this better be a life or death situation because I'm ..." he trailed off. He started shouting, "come on Cameron, get the damn ball and stop giving Dane a free pass just because he's the

Beta. I swear if you allow him to shoot another ball, I'll have your head for it!"

The volume of his sudden outburst startled Tasha. But she waited patiently while he shouted at his teammates before continuing their conversation. "Do mates feel each other's emotions because I think my emotions are a little high today?" She was starting to put two and two together after his outburst.

"Yes, they do. It normally happens when your mate's emotions are really strong. So right now, the overwhelming emotions you're feeling are because of my emotions," answered Alexavier.

His voice deepened as he growled before shouting, "Kate, is there a reason you allowed your mate to just walk past you with the ball? This is a competition! So whether or not he's your mate, you need to guard him."

Tasha could tell that Alexavier was having a very rough day. It made her feel bad for sending Zeus to the pack-house with Dane.

Once the office had cleared out, Tasha gave Derek the go ahead to lock all doors and activate the alarm. She then made her way to Alexavier's home.

Upon arriving at the entrance to his territory, she noticed a few wolves standing guard in the woods. Her eyes followed the few men and women dressed as guards as they walked up to the big gate.

The warriors had detected their Luna's scent from a long way off, before they caught sight of her car coming closer. When she stopped at the gate, the guards nodded in acknowledgement and the gate swung silently open.

Tasha overheard one of the female guards telling two of the wolves to show the Luna where to find the Alpha.

Alexavier sensed his mate the minute she entered his territory. Despite his desire to meet her, he was too distracted by the responsibility of coaching his team. Tasha's dog, on the other hand, was so eager to see her it couldn't wait until she was out of the car — it ran towards her with its tail wagging in excitement.

Tasha picked up Zeus the minute he was within her reach. Her fingers scratched behind his ears while he showered her with puppy kisses. She turned to the wolves that led the way and thanked them. Then she made her way over to where her mate was standing.

As the game drew to a close, she heard the anxious murmurs of the crowd as the tension built. She watched as Alexavier's eyes narrowed and his jaw clenched when Dane took the ball from his team member.

Everyone held their breath as Dane took the shot at the last minute.

It was as if time froze as everyone watched the ball roll around the hoop. The feeling of disappointment was palpable in the air as Team Beta watched the ball fall off the hoop.

Team Alpha members cheered and hollered in joy, and Alexavier's lips twitched in amusement at his brother's pout.

In her excitement, Tasha leapt onto Alexavier, and embraced him tightly with her legs. She had completely forgotten that she was still holding Zeus in her hand.

Alexavier's body melted into the comfort of his mate's warmth, embracing him. His hands instinctively flew to her waist, gently cradling her against his chest. He would have called it a perfect moment if her little puppy wasn't glaring up at him.

Tasha hurriedly unwrapped her legs when she realized what she was doing. She felt a wave of embarrassment wash over her as she stepped away from him, her eyes glued to the ground. However, she started choking on her saliva when she felt him wrapped his hand around her waist. She grinned as she felt the tingles from his touch, as he led them towards the dining area.

Tasha's mouth dropped open as she stepped into the vast dining area. But what had her shyness intensifying was the sight of the crowd's piercing gaze on her and Alexavier. Despite the general air of happiness, she noticed at least five or six people giving her a menacing look. Tasha's eyebrow arched inquisitively as she studied the small group. Her eyes twinkled, her lips curving into a smirk as she sensed the thrill of their challenge. Why do I feel like they're responsible for the rogues that attack me?

Tasha allowed Alexavier to lead her to the table where he usually dined at. She wasn't surprised to see the table in the center of the room, where he could easily monitor the movements of everyone. She noticed at least ten other people standing around the table waiting for them.

Alexavier felt his mate's nervousness increase at the sight of the people at his table. He used his thumb to make small, circular motions on the back of her hand to soothe her.

He'd also noticed that a few of the pack members were giving his mate death glares. His beast had sensed that something was up with the small group. Despite his anger, he resisted the urge to punish them while the pack was joyously celebrating.

When everyone was seated, Tasha's eyes widened at the sight of the women and men dressed in black and white, carrying out an array of different dishes. Her jaw dropped as she took in the vast spread of food, and her belly grumbled with eagerness. I am going to enjoy every bit of this.

She'd learned the names and titles of the people sitting at the table with her. To her right were Alexavier's parents, Itana, who she'd met before, and her husband Christopher Blu. Beside him was Sofie. Then Shane and his mate, Alisa. To the left of Alexavier was Dane, head warrior Kate and her mate Kevin. Then Gamma Shane's parents, Devon and his mate Talia.

Tasha was beyond full; it had been a while since she'd had that much food. But she was no match for the werewolves that surrounded her. Her little husky was just as stuffed as she was. Because he was lying on his back with his four paws in the air and his tongue was hanging out.

"Are you ready to go to bed?" Alexavier asked.

Tasha gave a silent nod as her hands found their way around his neck. She hoped he'd get her message that she was too full to walk.

The people at the table with her chuckled at the Luna's antics.

Alexavier couldn't help but to grin at his mate, but he was so thankful for her growing comfortability around him.

That night, Dianna's source told her where Alexavier's mate lived. She gave orders to two of her men to capture the human on the last day of the event. She wanted to be the one to kill Tasha, so she told them to bring her back to their home in South Carolina.

Dianna also planned to have her followers attack her old pack after she killed Tasha. She didn't reveal that part of her plan to them because it would be a suicide mission. She let out a dark chuckle as her smirk turned sinister. If everything went as she planned, she would become Alexavier's mate.

CHAPTER 22

After a long day at work on Thursday, Tasha went home and changed into her cozy black joggers and oversized hoodie. She picked up her overnight bag with all her necessities for the following day. Donning her Adidas sneakers, she hoisted Zeus off the floor and exited the apartment.

She was on her way to Alexavier's house to watch the soccer game finale. She was brimming with anticipation to watch her mate play his favorite sport. Knowing that Team Beta was up against Team Alpha.

As Tasha arrived at Blue Moon's territory, the guards bowed their heads in respect and allowed her entry. One wolf ran alongside her car, its paws pounding the ground as it led the way to the soccer field.

Alexavier felt a thrill of anticipation as he geared up for the last match. If his team won the event, they would win the overall sports event. Team Alpha was determined to take home the soccer trophy for another year.

Alexavier was elated to show his mate the agility of his soccer skills. His proud beast was radiating a dominant energy, which caused the pack members around him to show their neck in submission.

The scent of his mate alerted him of her arrival in his territory. He stepped out of the gym, feeling the rush of cool air on his skin as he went to greet her. The sight of her in one of his hoodies brought a smile to his face. Alexavier yearned to put his mark on her, but he had to wait until she agreed to be his. As soon as she was within his grasp, he drew her close to him. He planted a gentle, feather-like kiss on her forehead and neck.

Tasha shivered at the feel of his soft lips against her skin. The tingles that danced across her skin as his lips pressed against her neck had her biting back a moan.

As soon as he released his grip on her, she felt herself being lifted. She felt a thrill as the person spun her, the sound of laughter ringing in her ears. Her face lit up as she laughed along with him. She knew only one person had the heart to do that while Alexavier was present.

Alexavier growled at his brother, "be careful with her. You drop her and your momma loses a son." He could have ordered Dane to put her down. But he couldn't take his eyes off her, captivated by the sound of her laughter. It was like music to his ears and he loved it.

Sofie beamed with excitement as she saw her sister-in-law again at the event. She enjoyed spending time with Tasha. She giggled at her older brothers' antics.

Tasha turned around when she heard a small giggle. She smiled brightly, her eyes crinkling with delight as she hugged little Sofie.

"Where are the rest of the gang?" The gang comprised Mr. and Mrs. Blu.

"Mom and dad are in the house talking to Gamma Shane's parents," answered Sofie.

"I could bet my Porsche that they're in there talking about grandbabies," said Alexavier.

Sofie giggled. "Yep, that's the topic they were on before I walked out."

Tasha let out a cheerful chortle, enjoying the joyous atmosphere Alexavier and his siblings created. She could tell he had a deep love for his family and pack through the warmth of his interactions with them. She wondered if she was truly destined to run a pack with such an amazing man by her side.

Feeling the intensity of Alexavier's eyes on her, Tasha glanced up and returned his steady gaze with a shy smile. She hoped he wouldn't question the change in her mood. Gamma Shane's whistle broke the tension from his intense eyes, signaling the teams to prepare for the match.

She hugged Alexavier and whispered, "best of luck out there on the field."

She couldn't contain her laughter when she saw Dane's face scrunch in a pout after she refused him a good luck hug.

Alexavier flashed his brother a smug smile before sprinting to his team. "Alright everyone, this is the last game. We all know what winning this means for us. We would have the championship title in soccer and the overall title for the sports event. So let's go out there and show Team Beta why we are forever reigning champions!" shouted Alexavier to his team.

Team Alpha let out deafening cheers in agreement.

"Gather around Team Beta and listen carefully. We cannot afford to lose to Team Alpha another year while I'm team captain. So we are going to go out there and play our best. Today we show Team Alpha that their reign is over. Let's get out there and win!" exclaimed Dane to his team.

His teammates shouted, "hell yes!"

The players were ready, and the atmosphere was electric as the game commenced.

The crowd was a sea of contrasting emotions, with some people cheering and others growling in frustration.

Tasha would have been biting her nails in anticipation if she wasn't holding on to Zeus. A few minutes into the game, the sky had grown cloudy, yet the players and crowd remained undeterred. She was having a hard time keeping up with who had the ball due to how fast they were moving.

The sky lit up with a searing streak of lightning, and the ground shook with the ensuing thunder. A gust of wind sent dust flying in all directions, and the trees creaked and groaned as they swayed. Yet everyone stood silently, their eyes glued to the game, unable to turn away until the end.

Jay from Team Beta had the ball, and Kate from Team Alpha tackled him but was unsuccessful. His powerful kick sent the ball flying towards the goal. But due to strong winds, it went over the goalpost. All of Team Beta released a deep, guttural growl of displeasure. They were just two points away from victory.

Team Alpha's goalkeeper Ramon kicked the ball out, and Alex-avier caught it on his chest. He let the ball drop to his cleats and passed it to Ken on his left side. The game would be over in ten seconds. Alexavier freed himself from the defenders and made his way closer to Team Beta's goal. Eric passed him the ball and with a powerful bicycle kick, the ball went flying. It hit the far left post of the goal post before rolling into the goal.

The crowd cheered and whistled, the sound of their voices competing with the patter of rain.

Tasha and Sofie jumped up and down, squealing with delight and hugging each other.

Sofie didn't care who won. She was just there for the excitement and to watch both her brothers.

Tasha watched Alexavier carefully navigate his way out of the throng of people before she handed Zeus to Sofie. She ran to him and leapt into his arms, feeling a rush of joy as his fingers closed around her. She leaned in and pressed her lips to his, her heart beating fast as the sound of the crowd faded away.

As surprised as he was, Alexavier was quick to respond to the movement of his mate's warm lips on his. His wolf hummed, a low rumble of pleasure in his chest.

Tasha thought hugging Alexavier gave her a lot of tingles. But when their lips touched, it felt like her entire body was alive with electricity. Needing air, she slowly pulled back and opened her eyes. Her lips pulled into a teasing smile as she met his gaze.

Alexavier growled at her seductive look and her plumped lips. He dipped his head to kiss her again, the sensation of their lips locking, sending a wave of pleasure through him.

Everyone went to their respective homes to get ready for dinner. They were preparing for a big celebration the next day, in honor of the end of the events. Trophies and medals would be awarded to the team that won and to each member of the teams.

After taking a refreshing shower, Alexavier quickly changed into a pair of gray joggers and a comfortable white v-neck shirt. He waited in his room while his mate got showered and dressed.

Zeus bounded ahead of them as Tasha and her mate walked to the dining hall.

Tasha was looking forward to dinner with the pack. She was eager to satisfy her appetite with all the food that her belly could handle. All the anticipation and excitement made her famished.

Alexavier watched as his little mate stacked her plate with food. He was astonished by the amount of food his mate could consume, given her petite figure. But he loved it, especially when her eyes filled with joy at the taste of each dish.

The corners of his mouth turned upwards as she rubbed her tummy with satisfaction after she finished her food. He was thinking of taking her out on a date on Saturday, the day after the packs' celebration. He was planning to ask her out when he went to get her for the celebration.

"Hey, I'm ready for bed so I'm going to head up," Tasha said to Alexavier.

He got up from his chair and lifted her out of her seat, bridal style, instead of answering her. "Zeus, come!" called Alexavier.

The puppy barked happily and followed them up the stairs.

Alexavier used his foot to push his room door open. He placed his mate on the bed and stripped down to his boxers. "Zeus, you sleep on the couch."

Zeus wagged his tail happily and jumped up onto the couch.

Exhausted, Tasha couldn't muster the energy to argue with Alexavier about taking her to her room. She hoisted her hip, yanking her joggers off, and carelessly threw them in the direction of the wash basket. As she tried to find a warm spot in the bed, she felt a warm hand pulling her into a naked chest. Her breath hitched at the feel of his warm, muscular chest pressed against her back.

"Good night mate," whispered Alexavier, before he placed a light kiss on her hair.

"Good night Alexavier," Tasha whispered, feeling comfortable.

On Tasha's last day as boss, she took a deep breath of relief as she saw everything had gone perfectly. They worked diligently all week to complete the tasks they needed to submit by the end of the week. She was buzzing with excitement as she made her way home from work, thinking of the party she'd be attending with Alexavier.

The two male rogues that Dianna had sent out to capture Tasha sat in the bushes. They were waiting for her near her apartment building. They had parked the white van in the parking lot of the apartment, ready to take Tasha to the warehouse.

Tasha pulled into the parking lot at her apartment building and stepped out of her car. She clicked her keys to lock her car and turned to walk to the entrance of the building. However, her world went dark after taking only two steps from her car.

The rogue had hit her in the head with a piece of board. The man tried not to use too much force as he swung the board at the human. His leader had warned them to return with the female alive.

The other rogue effortlessly scooped Tasha up and carried her over to the van. He placed her in the back of the van and tied her hands and duck taped her mouth. He pulled out the cologne, spraying it liberally to mask her scent with its woodsy aroma.

The two males grinned as they pulled out of the parking lot. They had succeeded in kidnapping the woman for their leader.

Chapter 23

The seconds seemed to drag on for Alexavier as he watched the clock, waiting for the time to pick up Tasha for the party. He was nervous about asking her out and a little fearful that she would decline. What if she doesn't want to be an alpha's mate? His wolf whimpered at the thought.

He shook his head. "She wouldn't have kissed me like that if she didn't want to be with me."

He sat in his office chair, the sound of his pen scratching against the paper as he tried to get some paperwork done. He was flipping through the pages of documents that Tasha had handed to him the day before to pass the time. However, his beast was uneasy and on edge. He had been ignoring him, assuming that his wolf was just scared of potential rejection. But he was becoming increasingly frustrated as the beast inside him fought to be released.

Alexavier grabbed his phone to call his mate to appease his wolf. His eyebrows drew together in a frown as the phone kept ringing. He shifted the phone away from his ear to check the time. "She should be home by now," he mumbled. He called her number again, the sound of the ringing echoing in his ear before it stopped. On his third attempt, the call went straight to voicemail.

His emotions were starting to match the growing concern of his wolf. This was definitely not like his mate. He tried calling her again as he was leaving the pack-house, but all he heard was her voicemail. He ran his fingers through his hair, anxiety rising, before ringing his Gamma.

"Hello, Alpha," greeted Shane.

"Yo, Shane, meet me at the garage in two minutes." With that, Alexavier ended the call.

Shane frowned as he stared at his phone, perplexed. "That's different. I wonder what's up with him."

Alexavier then opened up the mind-link between him and Dane. "Bro, Tasha is not answering her phone. So I'm going over to her apartment to see what's up and I'm taking Shane with me. Take care of things here until we get back and don't say a word about this to anyone."

"Hello to you too, Alpha. Sure, I'll take care of things here. Just come back with our Luna," replied Dane.

"That's the plan. I'll update you if needed. Bye!"

"Later brother!"

Alexavier met up with Shane at the garage. "We're taking our motorcycle to avoid traffic."

"Okay Alpha," said Shane. He grabbed his keys for his black Honda motorcycle.

Alexavier kicked his red and black motorcycle to life, and the roar of the engine filled the air as Shane followed suit. As they took off out of the garage, the rumble of the engine echoed off the walls as they drove to their destination.

Alexavier couldn't remember the last time he'd ridden his motorcycle. But at a time like this, he was glad he still had it. Though he wished he could run there in his wolf form. It would have been much faster, but there weren't many trees in the city to cover them.

Alexavier and Shane rolled up to the apartment building and dismounted their motorcycles.

Alexavier began sniffing around to see if there was anything out of the norm. Not finding anything suspicious, he headed into the building to talk to Mr. Henry.

"Good evening Mr. Blu. What can I do for you today?" greeted Mr. Henry when he saw Alexavier approaching.

"Good evening Mr. Henry. I'm here to visit Ms. Williams. Is she up?"

Mr. Henry cocked his head and gave Alexavier a quizzical stare. "No, Mr. Blu, I haven't seen her since she left for work. I thought she went to visit you after work before returning." He began to feel concerned for the kind young woman.

Alexavier's worries heightened with every word, and his beast snarled in anger. He tried to smile at Mr. Henry. "Thank you, Mr. Henry."

With the hope of finding out where Tasha had gone, he made his way up to her apartment. Depending on the condition of her apartment, he could decide what his next move would be.

Using the extra key she offered him that morning, he was able to open the door. When he walked inside the room, the growing husky greeted him.

Zeus then made a mad dash through the opened door.

Alexavier raised a brow at the dog's unusual behavior. Something definitely happened to my mate.

Alexavier bent down and picked up the puppy, who was eagerly waiting by the elevator. He made his way to the parking lot to search for Tasha's car.

Upon seeing his Alpha approaching with the Luna's dog in hand, Shane pointed in the direction where his Luna's car was parked. "Her car is right over there and droplets of her blood are on the ground."

"Why didn't you call me as soon as you saw it," Alexavier growled out.

"I was hoping it was someone else's blood mixed in with her scent and you would return from the apartment with her in tow," replied Shane. He held his head down in submission, not wanting to piss off his already raging Alpha.

Alexavier snarled, as his claws and teeth started to lengthen. He walked over to the direction Shane had pointed, his teeth gritted and jaw clenched. He stepped up to the car, his nose in the air as he sniffed for any clues.

The smell of her perfume had grown faint and was starting to go away. He tried to detect any other smells in the air, but the smell of exhaust oil was too pungent. Without a scent to follow, it would be harder for him to track down the people that kidnapped his mate.

The air around Alexavier seemed to hum as he began to transform, his body trembling in rage. He hurried over to the woods, his breath ragged as he tried to remain undetected while shifting. He turned towards Zeus, his lips curled back in a snarl, as he commanded, "Sit!" Just as the trees covered him completely, his body curled as he morphed into his wolf.

Shane and every member of the pack could feel their Alpha's rage through the pack bond. The Gamma cautiously entered the forest to search for his Alpha. He walked with his neck exposed and hands raised. Hoping that the sight of his submission would prevent any attack from his Alpha.

Alexavier's wolf watched as the Gamma approached him. His body trembled with rage and his muscles were rigid with tension. A pleased rumble escaped him at his Gamma's submission.

"Alpha, I'm going back to the pack-house to get a search team ready," said Shane.

The alpha wolf gave a slight nod before trotting over to the whimpering puppy, his paws padding softly on the ground. He pressed his nose against the husky's soft fur and guided him toward Shane.

Shane got the message and picked up Zeus to take with him to the pack-house.

As his beast calmed down, Alexavier felt the sensations of his fur transforming back to skin. He rustled around in the tree and pulled out a pair of crumpled blue jeans and a white shirt.

For the purpose of being prepared for an unintentional transformation, werewolves often hide clothing in the trees.

He hurriedly threw on his clothes, eager to start conducting a thorough investigation. He went back into the building to talk to Mr. Henry. "I need to see the outside camera footage for today," said Alexavier as soon as he found the older man.

Mr. Henry's eyes widened at the deadly look in Mr. Blu's eyes. "Yes, Mr. Blu." Not wanting to piss off the Blu family, he motioned for Alexavier to follow him. He guided him down the hallway to the apartment's IT room.

Alexavier yanked open the door, the hinges creaking in protest, and Mr. Henry trailed behind him. The older gentleman's voice was gentle yet rushed as he explained the situation to the young security guard in the room.

As Mr. Henry spoke, the guard's eyes widened in dread. He glanced at the man standing behind Mr. Henry, and a chill ran down his spine at the fury in the man's gaze. He hurriedly replayed the video footage from the specified time they gave him.

The guard's trembling hands shook as he nervously shifted his gaze between Mr. Blu and the monitor. Fear gripped him, knowing that trouble would come if what Mr. Blu was looking for was of great importance. He was absent from the room for several hours, so he had no clue what had transpired to anger the man next to him.

Alexavier's eyes were glued to the screen, desperate to find out what had befallen his mate. Thirty minutes into the video, he heard the screech of tires as Tasha pulled into the parking lot. As she stepped out of her car, Alexavier felt a chill down his spine as two men approached his mate from behind.

From their attire, he knew they were rogues. Alexavier sat in silence, his body tense with the effort it took to control his emotions in front of the human. The next thing that happened in the video had the beast in him pounding against his mental cage. Its roars reverberated through his mind. His eyes kept changing from amber to gold as he helplessly watched his mate being abducted.

The guard's face was ghostly white as he watched the video. He had missed a woman being kidnapped while having sex with the new female guard. He wished he had taken his break instead of the guard who left before Mr. Blu's arrival.

The guard twisted his neck a bit to look at Mr. Blu and his face went a shade whiter. He could feel the heat of Mr. Blu's anger radiating off him. The man seated beside him had a white-knuckle grip on the arms of the chair, and his body trembled with fury.

"How the fucking hell did you witness a woman being abducted and not call the police? Or better yet, go out there to help her?" Alexavier asked calmly. The urge to break every bone in the guard's body grew as he stared at him. His wolf's snarl of agreement echoed through his mind.

"I... I... I... I ...," the guard stuttered out. He tried to think of any excuse to appease the man's fury, but his mind was blank. A chill ran through him as he felt true fear strike, and every nerve in his body screamed for him to run.

"You better hurry and explain because my patience is running thin. I don't have the fucking time to listen to you stutter," Alexavier said through gritted teeth.

"I.. I... I... wasn't in here when this... this happened, Sir." A strong desire to find a dark hole and hide overwhelmed the guard. The aura that surrounded Mr. Blu was nothing short of deadly.

"What the fuck do you mean you weren't in here? Then who the hell was?" Asked Alexavier. His temper was rising with every sentence the guard uttered.

"Um.... Um.. Well... Well, I was in the storage room with the other guard for the last three hours, Sir."

When he heard that, Alexavier felt his last nerve snap. With a single motion, he grabbed the guard by his neck and hoisted him out of the hair. "You mean to tell me there were no guards present? Correct me if I'm wrong, but shouldn't one of you be present watching the live feeds at all times? I guess you guys don't find this job important enough to take it seriously—"Alexavier laughed dryly.

"—I hope whatever it is you guys were doing was worth it." His lips curled into a sinister smirk as he grabbed one of the guard's hands and pulled it out of the socket.

The guard's eyes bulged, and he opened his mouth to scream. Alexavier stifled the guard's screams when he hurled him into the wall. He exited the room and gave a nod to Mr. Henry, who was sprinting towards the scene.

Alexavier's mind was filled with the growls of his raging wolf. His wolf was urging him to turn back and rip the guard's limbs apart. He quickly left the building before he really allowed his beast to do as he wished.

He felt the rumble of the bike as he pushed it to its limit, arriving back at the pack-house in less than thirty minutes.

Dane slowly made his way towards him, a solemn look on his face. "Shane and a few trackers went out to search the perimeter. They wanted to check if they could pick up her scent anywhere else."

Alexavier gave a slight nod of his head to signal that he had heard him. "Follow me to my office."

They made their way to his office. Members of the pack that were in the house hurried out of their Alpha's way.

"The other night I noticed Dianna's best friend Annie and her brother Dave looking at Tasha with a look of distaste. I need you to get them for questioning," said Alexavier. He sat in his office chair, his face devoid of any visible emotion.

He held up his hand to put a stop to his brother's incoming questions. "And before you even ask. I saw Annie sneaking out late at night ever since Tasha started coming around. Also, the rogues that had tried to kill Tasha a few days ago carried a familiar scent. That's why I am sure they are connected. So just go get them."

"Yes, Alpha." Dane rose to his feet and left the office to find the two people his Alpha wanted badly.

CHAPTER 24

Itana and Christopher walked into their son's office to see him staring out the window and drinking. When they both took a whiff of the air, they could smell the pungent aroma of whiskey.

Alexavier turned away from the window to face his parents. "I can't feel the bond, mom but I know she's not dead," he whispered. He clenched his jaw, trying to control the emotion that was bubbling to the surface and threatening to make his voice crack.

Tears rolled down Itana's cheeks as she ran over to her son to hug him. She felt a lump in her throat when she saw the hollow, desperate look on her eldest son's face. "From what you tell me and what I know, she's a fighter. We'll find her," she said in determination.

"I'll tell the pack that the party is off for now. I'll get everyone together and take care of things while you look for our future daughter-in-law," said Christopher. His hazel-colored eyes glowed as his wolf came forward to look at his pup. "Make sure you bring her home alive when you find her and give those rogues hell," he finished with a deep growl.

"Thank you, dad and mom," replied Alexavier.

Itana embraced her son tightly before leaving his office with her husband by her side.

Alexavier watched as Shane and the trackers walked out of the woods surrounding the pack-house. He placed his empty glass on the table and headed out of his office to greet them.

The pack members hastily stepped aside, their Alpha's powerful presence filling the air. His face was an eerie stillness, which was much scarier to them than the rage that was simmering beneath the surface.

Gamma Shane approached his Alpha. "There is no scent of the rogues in our territory or on neutral grounds. And there is no scent of the Luna either."

Alexavier growled, "figured as much after watching the video footage. It's obvious that they traveled in a vehicle and hid their scent. Unfortunately, it was parked in a blind spot at the apartment complex. So I was unable to get a license plate or a description of the vehicle."

Dane entered the conversation just as the Alpha finished talking. "I'm afraid you won't be happy with what I learned." He had a bad feeling about the people behind Tasha's kidnapping.

Alexavier's jaw clenched. He gave a slight nod to the trackers, signaling for them to leave.

They bowed in respect before turning away.

"Dane and Shane, let us talk in my office."

The three men walked into Alexavier's office.

Alexavier gestured towards the two empty chairs in front of his desk, inviting Shane and Dane to take a seat.

The three men had been best friends since birth. Even though Dane was a few years younger than Alexavier and Shane, he fitted right into the group. And Shane was more like a brother to the siblings.

"Annie's family reported that she left the house yesterday to go to class and didn't return. And according to Dave's mother, he left two nights ago and has not returned," said Dane.

Alexavier raised one eyebrow in curiosity. "And they have no idea where they went, and didn't think to report this to their Gamma?"

"Annie's parents made it clear this was the first time she disappeared without telling them. Dave's mother mentioned he's been acting strange ever since he got a call from his older sister, Dianna," answered Dane.

Shane's eyebrows shot up in surprise when he heard Dianna's name. "They were banned from any kind of communication with her, though."

"Exactly, so I confiscated her phone. The tech guys are working on it right now," replied Dane.

Alexavier stared ahead in thought. "If Dianna is a part of this, we need to find their location fast. Dane, go get another set of trackers and go into the city."

"Yes, Alpha."

"Shane, get a few warriors to watch Annie's family and Dave's mother."

"Yes, Alpha," agreed Shane.

"Alright guys, that's it for now," said Alexavier.

The Beta and Gamma left the Alpha's office to take care of their respective tasks.

Alexavier called a few of the neighboring packs to ask if there were any rogue sightings or sightings of a human woman. He told the other Alphas that rogues kidnapped his human mate. And he'd asked if they could inform him, if they found anything suspicious on or near their territory.

Dianna was pleased with her men for capturing the human without a problem. Now it was up to her to kill the woman. Maybe I should feed her flesh to the sharks in the ocean nearby, she thought.

She was curious about Tasha's beauty ever since she heard about her. She was too busy planning for their next move to get a glimpse of her when the men who had captured Tasha had brought her to the cells.

Dianna rose from her chair and the sound of her footsteps echoed through the hallway as she made her way to the basement. On her way to the cell, she thought back to the news she'd recently heard about the woman.

"Alpha Blu's mate showed up to the finale," Annie had said. She'd headed down to South Carolina after her college classes to meet up with her best friend.

Dianna had quirked a brow, wondering what was so special about that.

"She kissed the Alpha on the lips," Annie continued in a softer tone. She knew how in love her best friend was with the Alpha. Sometimes she felt like it was an unhealthy obsession, especially after learning Dianna was mated.

The sound of shattering glass had filled the room as Dianna's fist tightened around the cup. "She did what?!" Her eyes narrowed and burned with fury.

Annie's body had tensed as she backed into the wall, fear coursing through her veins at the sight of her unstable best friend.

Dianna shook her head, her mouth dry as she desperately tried to erase the memory. That night she'd spent hours in the woods hunting in her wolf form. Each of her prey was killed mercilessly as she pictured them as Tasha.

"Leader Dianna, can I help you with something?" asked the guard sitting near the holding cell.

Dianna's eyes snapped over to the guard. He was not as big as her other warriors. He looked like a teenager. "No, you can go get your dinner. You don't need to watch her anymore."

She then turned her dark gaze to the woman laying unmoving on the cold floor. She regarded the small woman with an unimpressed eye, taking in her every detail. What did he see in her?

The woman appeared fragile, lacking any backbone or strength. But she had to admit Tasha was pretty. "A little over average," she mumbled.

She stared at Tasha for a few more minutes. If she doesn't wake up in another day or so, I will have to wake her by force.

She closed her eyes and imagined the sight of the pack gathering around her, bowing to her as the rightful Luna. The corners of her lips twitched into a small smile as her eyes opened. "You shouldn't have entered our world, little human." Her lips curved into a cruel smirk as she sauntered away from the cell. "Your head is mine in a few days."

Chapter 25

Two Days Later

Tasha blinked her eyes open and surveyed her surroundings. She was in an unfamiliar place. What the hell happened to me? Where am I? she wondered. Her mind flashed to the moment she'd turned to head towards her apartment building. She cradled her head as agony surged through the back of her head from the recollection. She lay motionless on the hard concert floor with her eyes shut tight.

Her tight bun felt like a vise on her head, intensifying the throbbing from the hit she had taken. She gingerly touched her scalp, massaging her head in slow, soothing circles. A small groan escaped her lips when her hand moved to her neck where she felt dry blood. An indication that her capturer had hit her hard.

Tasha didn't know what day or time it was. The cell was dark, the only source of light coming from the small window, casting shadows across the floor. A window that was too high for her to peek through. Her body stilled at the sound of footsteps approaching the cell. She remained laying with her eyes closed and her breathing steady.

At the sound of something tapping against the prison gate, she cautiously opened her eyes. Her eyes connected with the man who was always glaring at her whenever she visited Alexavier. She stared at him; her face was void of any emotion.

"You don't look so high and mighty now. Where's that challenging stare you gave me back at the pack-house?" Dave asked with an arched brow.

Tasha lay in the same position, her neck turned to look at the man silently. The man was a part of the 'I don't like Tasha' crew. Do they plan on feeding me? She wondered. The mere thought of food sent her stomach into a flurry of growls. She closed her eyes, embarrassed by the gurgling of her stomach in the room's quiet.

"Answer me, bitch!" Dave growled out. He couldn't understand how a small human in a cold cell could be so calm. His wolf within growled at him for disrespecting his Luna. His wolf paced restlessly within his mind, not approving of his choice.

Tasha stared at the ceiling. She didn't feel like wasting energy talking to him. He obviously wasn't the leader. A dull ache pulsed in her head, and the sound of his shouting made it worse. All she yearned for was to be in the comfort of her home, embracing her puppy and mate.

"Did the man's blow render you mute?" he continued. He clenched his jaw as his face burned crimson with anger.

She raised her eyebrow at his ridiculous question. You wouldn't be making such comments if I was to knock you out, asshat.

Dave was about to say something but shut his mouth when he noticed his older sister approaching. He studied his sister's face.

She was no longer the jovial person she once was. Her hazel eyes were dark with hatred, and she lost control over the simplest things. However, she was still very overprotective of him.

"Is she awake?" Asked Dianna. She had been patiently waiting for the woman to wake up for the last two days.

"Yes, she is," replied Dave.

Dave and Dianna turned to face the cell and were met with the sight of Tasha sitting against the wall with an emotionless face.

Dave's lips curled up in a smirk. I see all it took for the little Luna to move was my sister's appearance.

"Finally awake, little human. It's time for me to have some fun before I put an end to your existence and become the rightful Luna," said Dianna. Her smirk was twisted and dark, like the coldness of her eyes.

"If you are after the Luna title, you don't need to kill little—old me to get it. I'll gladly hand it over to you. It's not like Mr. Blu and I are in some sort of relationship," replied Tasha. Her voice was nonchalant, but her heart cracked at the idea of losing her mate to another woman.

Dianna let out a low, dark chuckle. "You know little about mates and how the bond between them works. I would love to tell you how wonderful having a mate is, but I would be wasting my time. However, I will let you in on this small secret. The only way for me to get Alexavier fully is for you to be dead. And I can assure you that today is the day your journey in life ends."

Tasha let out a dry laugh. "If you think you can get away with killing me. You must have more screws missing than I initially thought after you started talking."

Instead of replying, Dianna opened the gate and walked in. She wrapped her fingers around Tasha's neck and effortlessly lifted her off the ground. Her grip was tight, her nails digging into the skin and drawing blood. "You don't get to talk to me that way. You are nothing more than a minor hurdle that I'll enjoy crushing."

Despite her oxygen levels depleting, Tasha refused to give the woman the satisfaction of knowing she had the advantage. She stared right into her enemy's eyes. Her eyes flashed with defiance when she retorted, "what too scared I could take you on in a fair fight even though I'm a mere human? Sounds like a pussy move to me." She leaned her head to the side in fake thought, the corners of her mouth twitching in a hint of a smirk. "If I were you, I would challenge my rival in front of the entire pack to prove that I'm better."

A snarl left Dianna's lips as she threw Tasha across the cell.

Tasha's body crashed into the bars before landing on the floor.

Dave grimaced as his wolf snarled echoed in his mind, not keen on watching his Luna get hurt. He made no move to help, even though his wolf was furious with him. While enjoying the show, he was surprised to see the little human kept fighting, despite the odds being stacked against her.

"I won't hesitate to end you, bitch. You should be glad I have other matters to tend to before I end your miserable existence. Best believe, I'll enjoy killing the mate of the man who killed my mate." Dianna glared at Tasha one last time before walking out of the cell. "Dave, let's go to my office. We need to finalize everything before killing her."

Tasha could hear a loud ringing in her ears as she slowly crawled over to the wall. She was positive that the impact from being thrown had broken a few of her ribs. "That crazy bitch cares more about my mate than her dead mate," she whispered. Why would she keep the man that killed her mate alive? Is she really that in love with him?

Sure she knew little about having a mate. But the small amount of time she spent with Alexavier had her craving for a lifetime with him. She felt like if she were to lose him to death, she would have been a walking zombie for the rest of her life.

Maybe even die from heartbreak.

It was at that moment, in the cell on the concert floor, Tasha realized she was already falling for Alexavier. "If I allow myself to die by that mutt's hand, I would never get the chance to confess my love to him," she mumbled. She closed her eyes, praying for the pain to ease so she could think clearly.

Tasha groaned as another wave of pain shot through her back. She gritted her teeth and attempted to lift her body from the floor. She scanned her surroundings for something that could help her escape.

I'm escaping this place even if I have to swim across the ocean.

She was about to give up when she remembered that she'd used pins to secure her bun for work. A soft groan fell from her lips as she reached up and pulled one pin free from her hair. She used the wall for assistance as she limped towards the gate. She tried to move as slowly as possible to not irritate her broken ribs. However, she tried to not let her broken ribs slow her down too much. Knowing she had little time to spare before the mutt came back to kill her.

She exhaled a deep breath of relief when she finally reached the gate. With each unsuccessful attempt to open the lock, her hope faded. The lock was nothing like the locks she'd picked back home. But she was relying on her basic lock picking abilities to work in her favor.

After struggling for ten minutes, she finally heard the satisfying click of the lock opening. She wanted to rejoice, but the throbbing in her body and haste of the situation stopped her. She listened for the sound of any approaching footsteps before cautiously walking out of the cell.

Dane had watched as his brother's fists clenched tightly, the only sign of his anguish over not finding a clue to Tasha's location. He was glad that his parents had taken over running the pack while they searched for the Luna. He had accompanied his brother for the past two days, looking for some kind of hint, but they had returned empty-handed.

His wolf let out a whine as he sat looking over the lake. He'd been running in his wolf form, trying to clear his mind. The two missing pack members had not shown up, which had helped to prove that Dianna was involved. Their scent was masked like the rogues, making it impossible for them to be tracked.

Dane was worried about his Luna's life. He knew Dianna had an unhealthy obsession with his brother.

He rose from the spot he was laying, feeling his muscles stretch and crack. He reluctantly tore his gaze away from the breathtaking view.

As he jogged back to the pack-house, he could feel his tension dissipating with each breath.

Alexavier stared at the empty glass in his hand. After the exhaustive investigation, they had yet to uncover any clues about Tasha's whereabouts. He was on edge, his body tensing up as two days passed without feeling the warmth of his mate. His wolf was clawing at the edge of his consciousness, threatening to take control.

His heart was aching for any sign that his mate was still alive. His beast's warning growl echoed in his mind, disapproving of his depressing thoughts. He closed his eyes to try to hold back the tears, a pained sigh leaving his lips.

A gentle pressure in his head made him open his eyes. The high-pitched yip of joy emanating from his wolf left Alexavier momentarily stumped. He jumped to his feet the moment he felt the pull from the bond.

The force of his movement caused his chair to crash into the bookshelf. He couldn't believe he could feel the confusion and worry radiating off of Tasha. Even though their bond wasn't as strong as before, he was thankful that the connection was still there.

Alexavier had a feeling that the bond was weak because his mate was miles away from his territory. He groaned as the urge to run in his wolf form became more vehement. He ran his hand over his face before leaving his office.

The alpha wolf stood at the top of the hill overlooking a lake at the edge of his territory. He'd felt the soft dirt beneath his paw as he ran through the forest, and his mind felt clearer with each stride. He lifted his head and howled into the morning sky. His howl was an agonizing melody of despair and yearning.

The members of his pack heard their Alpha's howl and joined in. The woods reverberated with howls as the members tried to comfort their Alpha.

Alexavier spent an hour in his wolf form laying at the top of the hill. As he lay there, he felt more emotions coming from Tasha. An intense wave of anger surged through him, causing his lips to curl into a snarl. Someone is about to feel my mate's wrath. Following the first burst of emotions, a light wave of fear and worry took over, causing him to stand up. He started pacing at the top of the hill as the uneasiness increased.

When he no longer sensed her fear, his wolf released a relieved sigh. Alexavier made his way back to the pack-house, hoping they would get a lead soon. He skidded to a stop as a wave of longing and desperation hit him. He felt the rumble of a frustrated growl rising from his chest. My mate needs me and I can't do anything. What kind of alpha am I if I can't even protect my mate?

He continued to run, the sound of his paws light as he made his way back to the house. His fur turned to skin as he shifted at the edge of the tree line. He grabbed his jeans shorts that he'd left behind a tree and got dressed.

Dane approached him. "Are you feeling a little better?"

Alexavier shrugged, savoring the relief he felt from the bond. "I can feel the bond, but it's weak. I feel like if we don't get a clue soon, I'll lose her," he whispered. He didn't want to have such thoughts, but his mate's emotions weren't giving him much reassurance.

Chapter 26

Tasha was willing to do whatever it took to get away from Dianna and her vicious wolves. With her life in jeopardy, she didn't have the luxury of waiting for her knight in shining armor to rescue her. She wasn't even sure he was aware of her abduction. When she'd failed to locate her cell phone, she figured Dianna's goons had taken it. She had no idea where she was, but she refused to sit around waiting for death.

She tried to move discreetly through the building. Her footsteps were light and quiet. She knew werewolves had exceptional hearing, as they were related to dogs. The pain from her broken ribs and her head was a constant reminder of why she needed to get away from them.

She remembered Alexavier mentioning wolves could track people by their smell. But the thought did not waver her determination.

I'd be damned if I died without fighting back.

Tasha climbed the stairs, trying to avoid stepping too heavy on ones that squeaked. She cheered herself on in her head as she approached the last step.

Her face contorted into a scowl when she saw a gigantic man. She muttered a string of curses under her breath.

The man's body was as big as the window he was looking through. His chest was bare of a shirt and was full of hair. He stood a foot shorter than her mate, but he had a lot of meat on him.

She bit her tongue to keep from screaming in frustration. Fuck it, I might as well go out with a bang. She took the last step and tried to tip-toe her way past the man. She groaned in annoyance when the floorboard squeaked, alerting the big man.

The rogue wolf turned to look at her and smirked at her facial expression. "Little miss, should you be out roaming?" He licked his hips as he ran his eyes over her frame.

Tasha's scowl deepened as the man continued to look at her as if she was a piece of meat. The man shifted his body slightly from the window and her eyes zeroed in on her escape route. She stood there, trying to figure out how to get past the burly creep in her way.

"I'm talking to you," he growled out through his crooked teeth. His teeth were as yellow as butter, and a few were missing.

She tilted her head to the side and rubbed her chin as if she was thinking of an answer. Her gaze darted around the area, searching for anything she could use to ward off the pervert. She smiled sweetly when her eyes landed on a nice size iron pipe a few feet away from where she stood. It doesn't matter how big he is as long as I hit him in the lethal areas.

The man ran his tongue over his lips again at the sight of her smile. He'd missed the dangerous glint in her eyes. His thoughts were filled with what he wanted to do to her body. "I like a submissive woman," he said in a matter-of-fact tone.

Tasha braced herself as she tried to walk sexily over to him. She stopped to pick up the pipe, and the man growled a warning. A small sigh left her lips as a wave of reassurance passed through her body. Alexavier? she wondered.

"Drop the iron and I'll forgive you. I'll worship that lovely body of yours too," he said, giving her a final warning.

Tasha's lips curved into a sly smile as she stared at him. "Over my dead body."

The rogue growled menacingly and lunged for her. She side-stepped him and swung the pipe onto his lower back. She gasped at the pain her movement caused her broken ribs.

The man slowly turned to face her, his eyebrow raised in question. "Was that supposed to hurt?"

Tasha flashed him a brief smile and shrugged. "I'm only human, after all."

Her smile momentarily mesmerized him, so she took the chance to swing the pipe into his reproductive area. The man wheezed in pain as he fell to his knees. She didn't hold back when she swung the pipe at his head before walking away as fast as could.

The sound of the rogue's body hitting the floor was the only thing she heard as she climbed out the window. She was overjoyed to have found a window on her first attempt. She did not want to risk walking around a place filled with rogues looking for an escape.

After a few moments of scanning for any wolves, she breathed in the scent of the fresh air. Despite the pain in her ribs, she was determined to put some distance between her and the psycho.

She took off into the woods surrounding the creepy building. She forced her body to move as fast as possible, despite her injuries. With no sense of direction, her only thought was survival. "At least I'm out of there," she wheezed out.

Tasha's ribs ached with every step she took, causing her to reduce her steady pace. She kept running nonstop until she got to a stream and drank some of its water to quench her thirst.

Even though her body begged her to rest, her determination kept her feet moving. She needed to survive so that she could beat Alexavier's ass for not telling her about his crazy ex. Everywhere she looked, the trees seemed to go on forever. She was completely isolated from the city.

She was still trying to make sense of the reality that the individual who targeted her — was a woman with an unhealthy obsession with her mate. She wasn't the type to pick fights with others.

Despite her best efforts, people always had some issue with her. To avoid unnecessary arguments, she tried her best growing up to keep her distance from women. Jade was the only woman that she kept close. The rest of her friends were mostly guys.

Tasha shook her head to clear her thoughts. She looked up just in time to see a wolf hunting a few feet away from her. From the size of the wolf, she could tell that it wasn't a wild wolf. However, she couldn't tell if it was a rogue or a pack wolf. She knew from her last experience that some rogue wolves had completely black eyes. And that they always looked dirty and unkept.

She didn't know what would happen if other pack wolves found her in or near their territory. So, instead of checking to see if he was friendly, she climbed a tree that was further from the wolf.

She perched on a sturdy branch a suitable distance from the ground, feeling the rough bark beneath her hands. She leaned her back against the tree and felt her muscles relax as she waited for the wolf to leave the area. As she closed her eyes to rest, she felt a wave of reassurance wash over her. She was exhausted and famished, her body aching for the much needed rest. She did not know if she was still in the state of Virginia or not.

After her nap, Tasha felt energized and ready to move forward. She didn't want to chance running into the wolf, so she jumped from tree to tree. She hissed as a wave of pain hit her in her ribs. Every jump made the leaves of each tree tremble and left her body aching in pain. She would stop to check if there were any wolves around before she continued.

She'd realized that her ribs were hurting less after her nap, and she was thankful. But her choice of traveling had the pain returning in full force.

If I ever get the chance to see that bitch again, I will surely give her a taste of her own medicine.

Dianna knew something was wrong the moment she stepped out of her office. Her best friend followed close behind. She was about to make her way down to the basement to kill Tasha. However, she could smell the scent of the human mixed with blood in the hallway. Why was her scent here?

Dianna hurried down the stairs to find her friend Jason. She'd instructed him to keep an eye on the human. She froze at the foot of the stairs as the scent of blood hit her hard. Her body shook in anger as she approached her friend's body. She let out a sigh of relief when she noticed the wound to his head was already healing. "Her injuries must have been the reason you're still alive," she mumbled.

She turned to face Annie. "Go alert the trackers."

Annie nodded and rushed back up the stairs to find the rogues that worked for her best friend.

As furious as Dianna was, she had to give the little human credit. She was impressed that the petite woman managed to defeat Jason. "It's amazing how all this time I was underestimating Alexavier's mate. The woman has more brains than she lets on," she murmured under her breath.

She heard a groan and looked down to see Jason stirring awake. She bent down to slap his face to wake him up fully. "Get your ass up. We need to find her fast before she nears any of the locals," she said with irritation.

Annie rushed back to inform her best friend that the trackers left to search for Tasha. She wasn't surprised that the Luna had escaped. She'd tried to warn Dianna, but she did not heed her warning.

"Follow me, we need to inform Dave and prepare for the worst-case scenario," said Dianna.

Annie nodded and followed her best friend back to the office.

Chapter 27

Crystal Pack

South Carolina

Alpha Reid sat behind his office desk, waiting for his warrior's patrolling details. He sighed, the sound of it muffled by the thuds of someone knocking at his door. Reid tilted his head in wonder as he caught the familiar scent of one of his warriors. "You may come in."

Greg rushed into the office but stopped short to give his Alpha a respectful bow. "Alpha Reid, while patrolling our eastern borders, I picked up a strange scent," said Greg. He was a young warrior in the pack, but was very good at his job.

Alpha Reid's eyes snapped up to the young warrior's face. It wasn't every day that he got news about something happening at the eastern border.

Greg continued, his eyes still lowered to the floor out of respect, "from the scent, I could tell it was a human woman. But she also smelled like a wolf, and a strong one at that."

Alpha Reid's forehead scrunched up in thought at the words, "wolf and a strong one." It wasn't regular for a human to carry the scent of a wolf. A strong wolf's scent would mean she was the mate of a gamma, beta, or alpha male. It had to be the woman Alpha Blu had called him about a few days ago, he thought.

What really concerned him was how the rogues had managed to sneak onto his land without alerting his warriors.

"Did you see her or know which direction her scent came from?" Asked Alpha Reid.

"No, Alpha, that's the crazy part. Her scent stopped a few feet away from where I was hunting. There is no road anywhere near the area where I picked up her scent either," replied Greg. The young man's face was creased with confusion. The woman's disappearance amazed him, yet he couldn't make sense of it.

Alpha Reid pretended to contemplate, his head bobbing up and down slowly. How is Greg such an excellent warrior but couldn't figure out the woman went into the trees? "I'll get the Gamma to look into it. You may go home, but do not mention this to anyone else," he warned.

He dismissed Greg and called for Gamma Willis. He also requested for a few of his trackers to join the meeting in his office.

Reid stared at people in his office before he spoke. He wanted to keep the situation discreet, so it was ideal if fewer people were privy to the details.

"Warrior Greg has picked up a human woman's scent close to our eastern borders. She could be the woman Alpha Blu had been searching for. It seems she went into the trees to stay out of sight of the rogues who'd captured her. While I contact Alpha Blu, I need you guys to go and see if you can track her down. You are free to kill any rogue that you spot around that area," ordered Alpha Reid.

"Yes Alpha," answered Gamma Willis and trackers.

"Do not return without her. You may leave," said Alpha Reid as he dismissed them.

"Yes, Alpha," they agreed before heading out of the office to find Alpha Blu's mate.

Alpha Reid let out a tired sigh as he rang Alpha Blu.

"Good afternoon, Alpha Blu," greeted Reid when Alexavier answered the phone.

"Good afternoon, Alpha Reid. How are you doing?"

"I'm okay. Could have been better. I have some news for you."

"I'm listening," said Alexavier. He was curious about the reason the Alpha of the Crystal Pack called him. He felt his heart racing as he prayed it was related to his mate.

"About thirty minutes ago, one of my young warriors was patrolling and came across a human woman's scent near our borders. It seems your mate is very smart because she went up into the trees. In order to stop people from finding her, including my warrior that was in the area. I have sent my Gamma and a few trackers to find her. When we get off the call, I'm going to send my Beta and some warriors to retrace her scent back to where she was being held," said Alpha Reid.

"Thank you for contacting me about this, Alpha Reid. I really appreciate it. My mate is not yet familiar with werewolves' law. So she might be hiding from your wolves and the rogues. She is very new to our world. I would like your permission for me and a few of my warriors to enter your territory tonight?" replied Alexavier.

"Permission granted. Call me when you're close by so I can have my men escort you to the pack-house."

"Thank you. I'll contact you when we're close. Bye."

"No problem, Bye."

Alexavier's hands trembled with fury as he slammed the phone down. "The motherfuckers took my mate to South Carolina." His eyes flashed gold.

His beast desired the blood of those that took away his mate. He was going to give every single one of them the death they deserved. The minute they had decided to touch what belonged to him was the minute they had signed their death certificate. He called for a pack meeting to inform the pack about what he had learned.

The pack figured something was amiss when the celebration party was canceled. Some wondered if the future Luna had finally rejected the Alpha. It had been a long time since they had seen her visit the pack, and it made them uneasy. Whispers were going around about the pack members that were also missing from the meeting.

As Alexavier's gaze swept across the field, his pack mates fell silent, the only sound being the wind through the grass. "Good afternoon everyone. I wish we were all gathered here for a celebration instead of a rescue mission. It seemed the rogues have up their game. They thought it was smart to mess with my mate and your future Luna. What they or the people that betrayed our pack didn't take into consideration is that my mate is strong and wise. I just received a call from Alpha Reid from the Crystal Pack regarding my mate's location. Her scent was picked up near one of their borders," Alexavier announced.

"I want four of my best trackers and twenty warriors to accompany me to South Carolina. We will end the rogues along with the traitors and bring back our future Luna—"

The pack growled in unison, the sound like a chorus of thunder. Fury surged through them at the thought of the rogues who had taken their Luna. They also felt betrayed by the members that worked with the rogues.

A lot of the warriors wanted to join the fight for the Luna. However, they understood it was not a fight on their territory, but another pack's territory. So they allowed the people their Alpha requested to step forward.

"Kevin, Vick, Sandra, Gregory, Jeff, Susan, Alexia, Cameron, Julisa, Steffan, and Grace. Jackie, Yin, Hallie, Justice, Andre, Eric, Shanique, Manii, Fie, Jin, Felicia, Jake, and Kihyun."

When the warriors and trackers that Alexavier called for stepped forward, he dismissed the rest of the pack with an order. "Starting tonight, curfew is in full effect until I get back. No one is allowed outside of their home after ten at night."

It was a rule set for Blue Moon members whenever the Alpha and his Beta left for business, war, or to visit another pack. The pack would be required to remain indoors after dark, under a strict curfew. Ten o'clock was the official curfew time.

Gamma Shane and the warriors that patrolled during the night were the only ones who were allowed out. When the Alpha and Beta were away, the Gamma was left in charge.

Alexavier told everyone to pack for at least three days before heading to his room to get his travel bag ready. The trip by car took them almost six hours to get to the South Carolina border. His body was tense with anxiety and he could feel the wolf inside of him—straining to break free. He wanted to find his mate and hide her away from the world. He knew his mate would never agree, but the thought of it soothed his wolf's anxiousness.

The warriors and trackers were proud of their Alpha's self-control. They knew if it was any other wolf, they would have been tearing the entire forest apart looking for their mate.

Alpha Reid stayed true to his words when Alexavier alerted him of almost arriving at their territory. A few guards were waiting to escort him and his team to the pack-house.

The bond was like a magnet finally finding its other half. The mate bond hit Alexavier full force the moment he stepped into the same vicinity as his mate. He struggled to contain his anger as he felt the onslaught of her emotions. He could feel his wolf's rage pounding against the walls of his mind. As much as he wanted to go find his mate, he needed to get more information from Alpha Reid.

Alexavier and his team followed the guards into Alpha Reid's pack-house.

Reid knew something was wrong when his trackers and Gamma hadn't returned. He was hoping he would have some news about Alpha Blu's mate's wellbeing. A defeated sigh left his lips as he walked out of his office to meet the young Alpha and his companions. He studied the group of people that entered his home.

The young Alpha's self restraint impressed him. He could tell that Alpha Blu was barely holding back his wolf. But Reid was glad that he had enough respect to meet with him first. "Alpha Blu and warriors, welcome to the Crystal Pack."

"Thanks for having us. Although I wish it was under different circumstances," replied Alexavier.

Reid nodded in agreement. "If you lot would follow me to my office."

The men and women followed the older Alpha to his office to discuss the situation. Inside the office, they all stood patiently waiting for Alpha Reid to update them about their missing Luna.

"I have sent my trackers and Gamma to locate your missing Luna, unfortunately..." Alpha Reid's body went rigid and his eyes glazed.

Alexavier watched the older Alpha closely. When Alpha Reid tensed, he knew the news the Alpha was receiving had something to do with Tasha.

CHAPTER 28

Tasha was about to leap to another tree when the snap of a twig gave away the presence of something to her left. She crouched low, praying it wasn't the rogues that had finally caught up to her.

The first wolf she spotted had a thick coat of dark brown fur. His fur blended into the darkness almost perfectly. She held her breath as the brown wolf sniffed around, his eyes fixed on the tree branches. The other wolves with him kept their noses to the ground, searching for any scents in the area.

She watched them carefully, waiting for them to turn in her direction. Her muscles twitched nervously as she waited to see their eyes. Ready to confirm whether they were wolves from a pack in the area. After her few run-ins with rogues, she somewhat knew how to differentiate the two. Pack wolves' eye color remained the same in both wolf and human form.

She did, however, realize that Alexavier's eyes changed to gold when his wolf was present. But she figured it was due to his eye color being so unique. I'll have to ask Alexavier about that when I get back.

The moment the wolf with the dark brown coat turned around, she knew he was from a pack. She was about to climb down to greet them when she saw the dark wolf's muscles tense up. She crouched lower and scanned the area for the incoming threat. Her eyes followed the other wolves as they approached the brown wolf, who looked to be their leader. From his height and build, she guessed he was a wolf with a higher rank.

She felt the vibrations of the fast-approaching paws and growls, and her head instinctively whipped in that direction. The rabid wolves had finally caught up to her. Even though she was unsettled by their ability to track her down so fast, she knew it was inevitable. After all, they were wolves. Look at the bright side. They caught up to me when there were pack wolves in the area. Maybe they'll be too scared of the pack to capture me.

Tasha watched as around twenty or more rogues entered the area. Dread replaced her enthusiasm when she saw the amount of rogues. She knew the pack wolves were seriously outnumbered, but she wasn't going to let them fight by themselves.

After all, the rogues were here for me.

She braced herself mentally for the upcoming battle. She prayed that even if she didn't make it out alive, the wolves that belonged to the pack would.

Her eyes darted from branch to branch, looking for one that could be used as a weapon. Her eyes lit up when she noticed a thick branch that was slightly broken. Knowing she couldn't break it without alerting the others. She announced her presence while breaking the branch from the limb.

"Now, now, ladies and gentlemen. Why would you want to fight the innocent when you are after this amazing lady? The one that broke out of your so-called prison. Did it cause your bitch of a leader to go ballistic when she didn't see me—where she left me?" By the end of her taunting, she had the branch gripped firmly in her hands. She swung it back and forth to evaluate how useful it would be in the upcoming fight.

Tasha surveyed her surroundings and noticed that all eyes were on her. The rogues snarled menacingly, their eyes narrowed in fury at her taunting.

Three of the rogues moved toward the tree she was in and circled it. She couldn't help but grin with satisfaction as the idiots did exactly what she was hoping for. Her gaze locked with the leader of the pack.

He studied her with an intense gaze, as if he was trying to determine if she was something extraordinary.

She had to acknowledge that she was not behaving in a manner that a sane individual would in her situation. But she had embraced the fact that she was not a normal human being long ago.

The Blue Moon Pack's future Luna intrigued Gamma Willis. For a human, she had a remarkable level of control over the situation. An outsider would have never figured out that she was someone new to their world. He could tell from her attitude that she was going to be a great Luna.

He reached out mentally to his Alpha to relay the situation and request reinforcements. He then mind-linked two of the trackers with him to return to the pack-house to guide the reinforcement.

Tasha watched the dark brown wolf waiting for a signal to attack. The moment his glazed eyes regained focus and his tensed muscles relaxed—she carefully made her way down the tree. She stopped at a thick limb that she could use as a safe point to launch her attack against the rogues circling the tree.

The three rogues snarled at her, their claws scraping against the bark of the tree, and she couldn't help but laugh at the sight. She perched on the branch, her feet dangling in the air. She then allowed her upper body to fall backward. Even though her ribs pulsed with pain, she refused to let it stop her from executing her plan. She used the area between her calves and thighs to grip the branch. This prevented her from falling while attacking the rogues under the tree.

The three rogues cocked their heads in confusion. They found the little woman's behavior quite weird.

Tasha used the confusion of the rogues to her advantage. She felt the satisfying thud of the branch as it connected with the nearest one. The impact sent the filthy gray wolf flying into the rogue closest to his right. With a thud, the rogue with the gray fur hit the ground and was out cold. The rogue, with its mottled brown and black fur, stumbled back in surprise.

The muddy orange coat rogue and the brown and blackcoat rogue lunged at Tasha simultaneously. She grabbed the limb just in time to pull herself back up. She groaned as pain pierced her in her ribs.

Maybe I should have just attacked them from the ground to avoid stressing my already aching ribs.

Taking advantage of the rogues' focus on Tasha, Gamma Willis pounced on the rogue closest to him. The trackers followed their Gamma's lead; taking out as many rogues as possible. After all, they were outnumbered and weren't skilled at fighting like their pack's warriors.

Tasha took in a deep, ragged breath before slowly turning to face the two rogues still snarling in rage at her. She felt a surge of adrenaline as she steeled herself for what she was about to do. Her movement came to a halt when she saw the dark brown wolf jump on top of the muddy orange wolf under the tree.

She felt a sudden surge of anger and her muscles tense as she leaped on top of the other wolf's back.

The rogue was so taken aback by her action that he stood rooted to the spot. By the time he had recovered from his shock, it was too late for him to try to shake her off.

Tasha wrapped her hands around the rogue's neck and squeezed, making sure to keep her grip firm. She prayed that her newfound strength would not fail her when she needed it the most. A few minutes later, she felt the wolf's body go limp beneath her, and she carefully climbed off.

She realized the burning rage she felt when she attacked the rogue was not her own. Which meant her mate was close by. The thought of her mate nearby spurred her on, giving her the strength to keep fighting.

She examined the battle, taking in the clashing of wolves and the whimpers of the wounded. She noticed that most of the rogues were dead or badly hurt. While the wolves that belonged to a pack had fewer deaths and a few injuries. This made her sigh in relief.

She felt something shift to her right, and the corner of her mouth twitched in amusement. She realized she was getting more attuned to her heightened senses.

The wolf lunged itself with a powerful leap, its jaws wide and sharp crooked teeth glistening with saliva. Tasha stood rooted with her branch ready. When the rogue was close enough, she sidestepped and swung the branch into the wolf's side. She smiled smugly as the rogue collided with the tree and the bark shook.

Before the rogue could get back up, she walked over to it and sent a powerful kick to its stomach. Her hands rose above her head with the branch and she slammed it on the wolf's head. She heaved, feeling bile rise in her throat as its blood splattered all over her.

With only seven rogues remaining, Tasha figured she could let the pack handle them. Every muscle in her body ached and her breathing was labored from exhaustion. Even though she wanted to keep going, her body had reached its limit.

She held her side, wincing in pain as she hobbled over to a tree away from the battle. She had to bite her lip to keep from screaming out in pain as she carefully lowered herself into a seated position. Just as her eyes started to drift closed, she saw a black blur dart by her and heard a sickening crunch.

Alpha Reid let out a tired sigh as his eyes regained focus. The news he had received from his Gamma was not one he wanted to relay to the young Alpha. "My men have located your mate and Luna, but rogues have also found her—"

Alexavier snarled, and his team responded with a chorus of growls at the news.

Alexavier was seeing red. He was out of Alpha Reid's pack-house before the older Alpha could finish talking. He shifted as he entered the woods surrounding the pack-house.

He gave his beast full rain, knowing that his wolf could track down their mate through their bond. He knew his pack mates were hot on his tail and wanted their Luna back home just as much as he did.

It didn't take them long to reach the area where the battle was taking place. Surveying the area, Alexavier noticed his mate on the ground by a tree. He could feel how exhausted she was through their bond. He heard a rustle of leaves, and his attention was diverted to a rogue creeping up on his exhausted mate.

In two steps and a mighty leap, Alexavier pounced on the unsuspecting rogue, showing no mercy. With a furious growl, he ripped the rogue's throat open. He dropped the dead wolf's body before turning to his mate.

He whined in his mate's ear, trying to wake her from her slumber. She sighed softly as she felt the chill of his wet nose against her warm cheek.

I know it took me a while, but I'm here to protect you, Love. Thanks for staying alive.

Chapter 29

The alpha wolf stood protectively over his sleeping mate as he watched his pack and the Crystal wolves search the area for any remaining threat. When the rogues were all dead, he shifted back to his human form. He did not care that he was sporting his birthday suit, as it was common amongst his kind.

Dane followed his brother and shifted before walking closer to where his brother stood protectively over Tasha.

Gamma Willis shifted and stood alongside Beta Blu so that they could hash out the details of their next step.

"Dane, I need you to take the rest of the team and track where those rogues came from. Alpha Reid's Beta should already be in the area. Notify me as soon as you locate them. I'll make my way there once I get Tasha to the pack doctor," ordered Alexavier.

Alexavier then directed his attention to the Gamma of Crystal's wolves. "Gather your injured and dead wolves and lead the way back to your pack house."

Both Beta and Gamma spoke in unison, "Yes, Alpha Blu."

Alexavier stooped to gather his mate into his arms, bridal style. He moved with caution, mindful of her injuries. As much as he wanted to seek revenge on the person who hurt his mate. He knew he had to first focus on getting her to safety.

He carried his mate back to Alpha Reid's pack-house, taking care to not jostle her too much. He had slowly come to the realization that any sudden movements would elicit an outcry from her. And caused her features to contort in agony. His mate's agony stoked the fire of his beast's thirst for the blood of all the rogues.

He tried to pacify his furious wolf by gently bringing his mate nearer so he could inhale her scent. She let out a small whimper that made him pause in his tracks.

It was a blur of trees as Dane and the rest of the team followed the scent that was leading them to the rogues' hideout.

As much as Dane wanted to rip Dianna and her group apart for hurting his sister-in-law. He held his anger in for the sake of being a sensible leader.

His chest puffed out with pride, knowing that his Luna was a fighter. He knew that in her situation, most people would have stayed captured, awaiting death. His sister-in-law was a beacon of perseverance in the face of adversity, never wavering in her will to survive.

He recalled his interview with her. That was when he first realized that she was a born leader, just by the way spoke and carried herself.

He could picture the hell Tasha gave those rogues. Even he had to admit that she was a force to be reckoned with when she was angry. He had witnessed it firsthand on more than one occasion.

Dane slowed to a jog when he sensed Alpha Reid's Beta. Signaling the others to follow him to where the other Beta stood, waiting. He gave the other Beta a nod of acknowledgment, seeing that they were both in wolf form.

Dane untied the shorts he had bound around his leg and shifted back to his human form.

The other Beta followed suit while the other wolves waited in their wolf form.

"My name is Travis White. Nice to meet you. My trackers and I have followed your future Luna's scent to an abandoned building a mile from here. About three or four rogues are guarding the front entrance and another five are around the back. Two rogues on the roof. We can't tell how much is on the inside and we can't scent them out because they hid their scent with some kind of incense."

"Are there any side windows or trees close to the roof?" Asked Dane. He was thankful they were carrying out the operation at night. The darkness provided them with a bit of cover to move around with less detection.

"It appears that the windows have been boarded up, but there are trees that are very close to the roof," answered Beta White.

"We can use the darkness to our advantage. If we want to get in unannounced, we are going to have to take the trees up to the roof. Take out the rogues up there before going in," replied Dane.

He paused, and the air was thick with tension as he looked at the group. "I want two trackers to head back to the pack-house to get Alpha Blu and another three trackers on the lookout for any other rogues in the area. Also, ten warriors will wait near the building until we take out the rogues in the front. The rest of us are going up to the roof."

Everyone nodded in understanding. The two trackers left and the other three went to scout out the area for other rogues. The rest of the team jogged closer to the rogues' base and hid behind bushes.

Beta White waited with ten of the warriors while the others went for the trees.

Dane stressed the importance of being quiet and warned that they should only shift into their wolf if in a perilous situation.

Dane and his team grabbed the tree, slowly climbing until they could just make out the top of the roof. He motioned for the group to stay put, and then crept over to the roof.

One of the rogues heard the branch beside him shake, but he brushed it off as nothing more than the gentle rustling of the wind. What he failed to notice was the guy now standing behind him.

Dane wrapped his hand around the rogue neck and snapped it before slowly laying him on the roof. The wind blowing in the opposite direction made it easier for him to sneak up on them without being scented. Moving to the second rogue and doing the same. When he was finished, he waved his arms in the air to beckon the others to join him on the rooftop.

Jin opened the door on the roof that led to the inside of the building. Everyone stepped cautiously, the boards creaking like an old woman's bones with each movement. Everyone's senses were on high alert. They advanced cautiously, wanting to keep their presence hidden until they could determine how many rogues were around them.

They arrived on the second level, where they finally encountered three rogues guarding the stairs that led to the first floor.

Dane signaled to two of the warriors to take them out and turned to the others to guard the other doors.

Once all three rogues were dead, Dane and the others continued their journey to the first floor. They were in a heightened state of alertness, with ears tuned for the slightest sound of any kind of movement.

When Dane opened the front door, he felt the chill in the air as the rogues turned to see who it was. Before the rogues could react—Dane, Felicia, and Yin reacted with deadly strikes that killed them in one blow. However, they failed to notice another rogue running to set off the alarm.

It was only when the alarms started blaring that they realized their miscalculation.

Dane's growl filled the room, a deep rumble of irritation. In an instant, he was behind the male rogue. His claws gripped the man's throat before he sunk his fangs into the man's neck. Blood dripped from his lips as he spit out the chunk of flesh he'd rip out. He dropped the dead rogue and waved Beta White and the others over to the building entrance.

CHAPTER 30

Dianna tensed at the sound of the alarm blaring through her home. She was out of her office barking orders to her followers with a speed that took them by surprise. Her eyes connected with her brother's and she signaled for him to follow her.

She was furious that the wolves she had sent out to capture the little human had failed. And instead, had allowed wolves from the pack to enter her domain. She didn't think it was that hard to catch a mere human. They were werewolves, for crying out loud and she had badly injured the woman.

One thing she was certain of was that if the pack had arrived, then Alexavier was close by. Her goal was to be his mate, but if he found her now, she was as good as dead. Her new goal was to escape and plan her next move.

The first floor was filled with her dead followers, and blood was splattered on every wall. She glanced around and could see some people engaging in combat in their wolf forms, while others stayed in their human forms. She cast a wary glance around to check if

Alexavier was around before heading out the front door—with her brother hot on her heel.

Even though she wasn't the most competent leader, Dianna had developed a deep bond with the rogues. They had accepted her when she had been cast out.

Upon discovering that Tasha had escaped, she'd made the decision to send Annie out for reinforcement. She knew that if Tasha had somehow encountered Crystal Pack's wolves, then they would all be in a lot of danger. She didn't have a large group, and she had already lost her mate along with some of their strongest fighters. So, she knew her pack of rogues would be outnumbered if another pack found them.

Dianna had no idea how far their reinforcement was, but she knew the urgency of the situation.

Her brother was all bark and no bite—he might have seemed tough to outsiders, but he was no fighter. The only way for them to survive was to flee, unnoticed in the darkness.

Alexavier stayed in the hospital long enough to watch the pack doctor examine his mate's injuries. He was overwhelmed with anger when the doctor informed him that Tasha had suffered three broken ribs and a mild concussion. He roared as slammed his fist into the wall, leaving a dent in the plaster. His wolf was relentless in its clawing and snarling, demanding to be released.

His wolf's features were evident, with lengthened canines, glowing gold eyes, and lengthened nails.

Protect mate. Were the only words running through his mind.

The doctor took small steps back as the Alpha's kill intent surrounded the small room. He knew it was a bad idea to stand in the way of a furious alpha male.

Alexavier slowly walked over to the bed his mate was sleeping in and tenderly planted a kiss on her forehead. He stormed over to the door and paused, taking one last, lingering look at her. "Take good care of her, Doc."

On his way out of the small hospital building, he noticed the Gamma waiting. He approached the man, still not knowing his name.

Gamma Willis turned to face Alpha Blu when he felt his presence. He bowed in respect.

"What is your name?" asked Alexavier. His voice was a guttural growl, a clear indication that his wolf was present.

Gamma Willis's head shot up in surprise. "My apologies Alpha Blu. I should have introduced myself earlier. My name is Blake Willis. Nice to meet you, Alpha Blu."

Alexavier gave a curt nod. "Thank you for protecting my mate while I wasn't around. Watch over her once more while I handle the rest of the rogues."

"It would be an honor to keep watch over your Luna. After all, she fought alongside us, even though she was in pain." Gamma Willis's chest swelled with pride knowing that the Alpha of a great pack thanked him for doing his job.

The two men turned to face the woods at the sound of approaching paws. A light brown and a white wolf burst through the trees.

Alexavier's gaze lingered on each wolf, searching for signs of injury.

Jake and Hallie had come to collect their Alpha, the moonlight glinting off their fur. They bowed their heads in reverence to their Alpha before gesturing towards the woods for him to follow.

Alexavier transformed into his wolf within seconds and opened up the mind-link with Jake and Hallie. "What's the status, guys?" he asked, while running beside them.

"We found an abandoned building east of here. Beta Blu sent us here to get you. We are still unsure of their numbers because their scent is hidden," answered Jake.

Alexavier nodded his head in acknowledgment before telling them to speed up. He planned to return to the hospital before Tasha woke up.

They arrived just in time to see Dave and a female sneaking out of the building. He could smell the stench of blood surrounding the place. His eyes remained focused on the two figures trying to get away unnoticed. He released a powerful growl that made the ground tremble beneath his paw.

Dianna's steps faltered as a menacing growl filled the air, shaking the earth beneath her feet. At the sound of the predator, the birds scattered from the trees. Her brother started whimpering and she could have sworn she scented his urine. She wrinkled her nose in disgust. But instead of addressing her brother's reaction, she spun around and her eyes locked with the wolf she was in love with.

Alexavier watched as the woman's body tensed. Although smaller than Dave, she stood protectively in front of him. Her skin tone was lighter than Dave's. She was draped in black leather, from her pants to her jacket. Her ginger-colored hair was pulled into a neat puff.

He smirked in satisfaction as Dave's whimpers filled the air. He would have let out a dark chuckle if he was in his human form when the scent of the pup's urine filled the air.

"Hello Alpha, nice to see you again," spoke Dianna while trying to cover her much taller brother with her body.

The alpha wolf's fur bristled at the voice of the woman who had tried to mark him in his sleep. His low growl filled the air as he watched her every move. The way she looked at him had not changed, and it made him shiver in disgust.

He couldn't believe Dianna still had feelings for him, despite all the time that had passed. He had hoped she had enough sense than to mess with an Alpha's mate, but it seemed he was wrong.

The alpha beast slowly stalked his prey, his eyes trained on Dianna as she backed away. His eyes blazed with fury, but his steps were calculated and controlled, like a predator savoring the hunt. He licked his sharp fangs and crouched low, preparing to pounce. Those that betrayed him and his pack were going to feel his wrath.

Dianna kept her face neutral as she prepared herself for Alexavier's attack. When she saw him flying towards her, she waited until he was close enough to yell a quick "duck!" to her brother.

She sidestepped the alpha wolf and pulled her small pistol from her pocket and fired a few rounds at him.

Alexavier whimpered as the bullets pierced him in his shoulder and side. He fell hard on his side. The excruciating pain let him know he was hit with silver bullets. He struggled to get back up, loathing the thought of dying by the hand of the woman who had hurt his mate. However, the silver was spreading through his body at a very fast rate. He bared his teeth and growled in frustration; the sound reverberating in his chest.

"We could have had something special. We could have been a very strong and beautiful couple, but you kicked me out of the pack. You even made it worse when you chose that stupid, weak bitch as your mate," said Dianna as a dark chuckle fell from her lips.

Alexavier let out a low, menacing growl in response to her disrespect towards his mate. He was straining with all his might to lift himself from the ground.

She smirked at him and was getting ready to send a kick his way, but froze because of her brother's high-pitched scream. When she heard the sound, she turned to find a light brown wolf dragging her brother by his ankle. She raised her pistol, her finger steady on the trigger as she pointed it at the wolf. But before she could pull the trigger, a dark brown wolf flew at her from the woods.

CHAPTER 31

Moments before Tasha and Blake arrived at the scene...

Tasha jolted awake, startling the nurse, who was taking her vitals. Her eyes surveyed the room until they landed on the nurse, whose face was twisted in astonishment. "Where is my mate, Alpha Blu?"

"Um, Miss Williams, he went to the rogues' base of operation," answered the nurse.

Tasha ripped the IV needle from her hand and was out of the small bed the minute the nurse finished speaking. She could sense that something was amiss, and she knew she had to find her mate quickly. She gritted her teeth against the pain in her ribs and head.

"Miss, you can't leave. The Alpha gave us strict orders to make sure you stay in bed while you heal," said the nurse.

Tasha's gaze lingered on the nurse for a moment before she shook her head and walked out the door. She silently prayed that someone would be kind enough to take her to her mate, and fast.

Gamma Willis saw Miss Williams rushing out of the room they had her in and approached her. "What are you doing out of bed, Miss Williams?"

"I need someone to take me to my mate. Something doesn't feel right," replied Tasha. She watched as the older gentleman nodded before turning around and telling her to follow him.

"By the way, my name is Blake Willis. Gamma Willis at your service, Miss Williams," said Blake as he led her outside. He made his way behind a tree to shift.

Tasha's eyes widened as the dark brown wolf that had helped her fight the rogues stepped from behind the tree.

He lay down on the ground, and with a nod, motioned for her to hop onto his back.

She eagerly complied, her eyes filled with joy.

Shots rang through the forest as Tasha and Gamma Willis approached the rogue's location. Her heart stopped short at the sound of a wolf's whimper.

"Please hurry," she pleaded to Gamma Willis while praying that Alexavier wasn't the one who got hurt.

She held onto the wolf, feeling the power of his muscles flexing beneath her as he moved faster. She felt her hands tighten around his fur as he lunged into the air.

Gamma Willis's jaws snapped shut around Dianna's hand, that held the pistol, making a loud crunch.

A scream rose from the depths of Dianna's throat. A good chunk of her hand was ripped off from her, trying to dodge the wolf's attack.

Dave fainted at the sight of his sister's blood.

"No, no, no," mumbled Dianna as she stared at the remains of her arm in disbelief. Her voice rose as the realization sank in.

Tasha hopped off Gamma Willis's back as soon as he skidded to a complete stop. Her heart sank as she saw her mate lying on the ground, whimpering in pain. Blood flowed from the areas where he was shot. "I thought you people healed fast. Why isn't his wound healing?"

The first set of tears fell as she rushed to his side. "Get help now!" she shouted. She ran her hands through his fur, trying to find any more hidden wounds. She couldn't lose him now. Not before she could confess her feelings for him.

Tasha heard fast-approaching footsteps and turned to see Dane and a few others rushing toward her. She did a quick check over their bodies to make sure they weren't badly hurt.

"Dane, tie that bitch up before she tries to escape. Kill anyone that worked with her," Tasha ordered.

Dane gave a curt nod to his Luna before barking out orders to the others. As much as he wanted to check on his brother, he knew his Luna could handle taking care of her mate.

"Alexavier baby... please... Please... please stay... do... don't die on me," cried Tasha. "I.. I.. I... can't lose you, I promise to be nicer to you. I won't allow Zeus to bite you without a reasonable cause." Her lips trembled as her wolf emitted a heartbreaking whine.

She couldn't recall the last time she cried so much. But with her mate on the brink of death, she could barely breathe. The pain of losing him was so strong, it felt like her chest was being squeezed.

It felt like a lifetime, but she knew it was probably thirty minutes before the pack doctor finally showed up. "Doc, please work around me. I want to be by his side to bring him comfort," she pleaded with the pack doctor.

The doctor nodded in understanding before getting to work.

Dane sensed the change in Beta White while he was checking to make sure the two prisoners were secured. He walked over to where the other Beta was standing.

Beta White intently listened to the reports of his three trackers, who had been sent to scout the rest of the area surrounding the building. He turned to face Beta Blu. "We have rogues coming in fast from the northeast. The trackers aren't sure how many."

Dane nodded, he then signaled to the rest of the team to head northeast. "Stay low and alert," he warned.

Annie hoped she wasn't too late with their backup. Her step halted as the scent of her pack mates and other wolves surrounding their base. She signaled with a nod of her head for the others to slow down. She walked over to a tree that was big enough to cover her while she changed back to skin. "I can smell pack wolves close by. We need to move in stealth mode so that we can get my best friend and her brother out of there fast."

The rogues let out deep growls of agreement before continuing on their path.

Dane perched atop a tree, an amused smirk playing on his lips as he watched the approaching rogues. With a flick of his left hand, he signaled for the wolves on the left to attack. He did the same thing with his right hand. He waited to see who would run before signaling for the wolves that were trailing the rogues from behind.

Annie's chest rumbled with a deep growl when she realized the pack had them surrounded. She knew they would not escape without a fight. The hair on the back of her neck stood at attention at the feel of something deadly approaching.

Dane snarled, his voice rumbling like thunder as he slowly approached the traitor. He hated traitors, especially the people that betrayed their pack. He circled his prey, his muscles tensed and his sharp teeth bared.

He watched as Annie's eyes widened with fear, her body shaking as she took a step back.

He lunged forward, and she felt the slight gust of wind as she rolled away with agility, her small frame slipping out of his reach.

Dane turned just in time to see her lunged for his hind leg. He managed to narrowly avoid her attack. He faked like he was going after the left side of her neck. But swept his claws at the right side of head, ripping off a piece of her ear.

Annie's heart raced as she watched her Beta, a soft whimper escaping her jaws. She knew she couldn't win, but she wasn't going down without a fight. With that thought, she lunged for his throat but at the last second bit into one of his front legs. She gave a wolfish smirk when she heard his whimper. She shook her head and hurriedly stepped back before he could swipe at her throat.

Dane had to give the girl some credit for the move she'd pulled. However, his front leg being hurt wasn't going to stop him from ending her. He waited for her to make the first move, and when she did, he dodged and dug his claws into her side.

His chest rumbled with satisfaction when he saw her fur and blood on his claws. He didn't give her a chance to recover as he lunged for her. His sharp teeth gripped her by neck before he threw her into a tree.

Annie let out a loud whine as the impact jarred her body. Gritting her teeth in determination, she tried to fight through the pain as she forced her legs to stand. Her body felt weak, and she could feel the blood flowing from the wound on her neck. She tensed when she felt her Beta's presence by her side.

His lips curled in a menacing snarl as he looked at her. Her blood mixed with his saliva dripping from his jaws. Then he went in for the kill; ripping out her jugular.

CHAPTER 32

Three days had gone by since Tasha escaped from Dianna's clutches. Even though the battle against the rogues was over, the battle to keep her mate alive was still ongoing.

Alpha Reid had kindly opened up his pack-house to the team.

The team longed to return to their own territory, but they had to stay in South Carolina, as their Alpha had fallen into a coma.

Tasha sighed, her heart heavy with the memory of Dr. Hart's words. The doctor had informed Dane and her that Alexavier had slipped into a coma. And that there was no telling when he would wake.

"It's a good thing we got him back here when we did. A minute later, he would have died due to how fast the silver was spreading. Fortunately, we got it out of his system before it got to his heart," said Dr. Hart after the surgery.

Tasha tried to control her emotions, but the tears kept flowing, despite her efforts. She was so close to losing the man that had been a part of her dreams for many years. The harsh truth intensified the pain in her heart.

The intensity of her anger towards Dianna was like a searing heat. A heat that seemed to grow stronger with each passing day that her mate was in a coma.

The sudden creak of the door opening jolted her out of her chaotic thoughts. She watched as Dr. Hart approached her with a warm smile. He was a handsome man, even with the few strands of silver here and there in his dark hair. He was tall, with dark chocolate skin and lean muscles. She attempted to smile through her tears, her lips quivering with emotion.

"Luna Williams, I need to check on your injuries," said Dr. Hart.

She gestured to him with a nod, indicating that she was okay with him examining her wounds. She had forgotten about her own injuries.

Dr. Hart instructed her to lie down on the bed that was on the other side of the room. He checked on her ribs and her head injuries. "Please try not to move around too much. I will instruct Nurse Toya to bring some painkillers," he informed her.

"Can you help me move this bed closer to his?"

"Sure." Dr. Hart moved the bed for her, the wheels squeaking against the floor.

"Thank you, Dr. Hart. Sorry for being a burden," said Tasha.

"It's my pleasure and you are no burden to us."

After Dr. Hart left, Dane entered the room. He gave her a quizzical look when he noticed the way she had arranged her bed.

"Not a word!" She warned.

He raised his hand in surrender. "I didn't utter a word."

She rolled her eyes at him as she settled next to Alexavier. She slightly winced when she moved because of a bit of discomfort.

Dane rushed to her side. "Are you okay?" His forehead furrowed as his eyes carefully scrutinized her frame.

She smiled and fanned him off. "I'm okay, just a minor ache." Her words did not ease his worries. She tried to change the atmosphere by switching the subject. "How's everyone? Did you check in with Gamma Shane?"

"Everyone is doing okay. The few who got injured have already healed. Shane informed me that everything was running smoothly at home. He also reported that he has been going to the company to check and everything was good there. The only problem we all have is when the Alpha is going to wake up. Mom and Dad are worried and want to come down here. I tried to ease their worries as best as I could."

Tasha gave a brief, solemn nod, her lips pursing in understanding. She had been worrying about the pack. She was glad that they didn't lose any members during the battle. "I think you guys should head home. At least the pack will feel more at ease with you there. I'll take care of him. We will head home once he wakes and Dr. Hart agrees he is good to travel."

Dane tried to argue, but she raised her hand to stop him. "I know it's your job to protect us, but the pack and company need you too, Dane."

He released a long, heavy sigh of defeat. "Fine, I'll inform the others about our departure, but you have to keep me updated every day."

She gave a gentle, comforting smile. "Of course." Her expression changed to one of seriousness. "No one is allowed to lay a finger on Dianna and Dave until Alexavier and I get back. Let the others know they are only to be fed bread and water once a day."

"Yes Luna."

"I don't mind if you break a few bones if Dianna disrespect you. But no one else is allowed near her. We don't know who else is working with her. I would be very pissed if I returned and she's missing."

He nodded, his expression one of understanding. A soft smile played on his lips as Tasha continued to showcase her Luna instincts.

At around mid-day, Dane and the others started to prepare for their trip home.

Tasha watched from the steps of the pack-house as Kevin and Yin pushed Dianna out of the prison building.

Dianna passed by her with a smug smirk on her face, as if she was the one who had come out on top.

Tasha's laughter filled the air as an unsuspected Dianna bumped into the car door.

When they were all set, Tasha smiled and waved goodbye to the group. "See you soon and I promise to keep you guys updated every day."

Once the three SUVs were no longer in sight, she walked back to the room she and her mate shared.

She found comfort in resting her head upon Alexavier's chest while lying next to him. She closed her eyes and let the steady beating of his heart soothe her as she fought back her tears. Her lips started moving as words stumbled out to keep the tears at bay.

"You know when I first saw you that day at work? I was thinking to myself, what kind of sorcery is this? I mean, could you blame me? My dreams never came through until the day I walked into your office and saw you staring at me. You know, when I escaped, I was determined to make my home so I could knock the lights out of you for not telling me about your crazy ex. But you just had to go get hurt before I could hit you." She let out a dry chuckle.

"When I saw you laying there on the ground in your own blood that day. It brought me back to the day I lost both my parents. They died in a car crash. The stupid driver was too high in the clouds to see that the light was on red. It happened during my sophomore year in college. That semester, I wanted to give up on my dreams. But I kept going because I knew they wouldn't rest in peace if I did. As you probably figured out by now, I'm an only child. My dad had a soft spot for me. I spent most of my childhood learning the different parts of a car. At the age of eleven, I could assemble a car engine and I was very proud. I didn't mind spending all my days with my parents because I was too shy to make friends. My mom would laugh every time I walked into the house with some type of oil on my forehead. I was also very close to my mom. She was there when I needed someone to vent to. Everything I know about fashion came from her. She didn't teach me how to cook though because I didn't have the patience to watch a pot. But I picked up a few things from both her and dad," whispered Tasha.

She coughed, her throat feeling strained and raw. "I know you think I'm strong and independent and don't get me wrong, I am. But it gets tiring sometimes. I want to be treated like a queen and be able to depend on someone other than myself and best friend. You may not have realized this, but you have somehow attached yourself to my heart. So losing you would hit me just as hard as when I lost my parents. You make me feel things I didn't believe were possible. Things that scare and excite me at the same time. You need to wake up, Alexavier. No, you must wake up, mate, because I am barely holding on to this reality. I miss your voice, smile, and the way you always want to protect me."

She lifted her head from his chest, her fingertips tracing the contours of his jawline as she studied his face. Her lips curved upwards in a warm smile when she felt the familiar tingles.

There was a faint knock, and she reluctantly lifted her face from its place nestled against his chest. "Come in," she called softly, knowing the person behind the door could still hear her.

Tasha watched as Toya, the nurse whose name she finally learned, stepped into the room with a tray of food in hand.

Toya was a small woman, she was a few inches shorter than Tasha. Even though she was petite, she had curves in all the right places. Her skin had a nice caramel tone and her hair flowed like a waterfall, brushing her hip as she walked. All in all, she was another beautiful werewolf.

"Thanks, Nurse Toya," she said after Toya had placed the tray by the table near the bed.

"You're welcome, Luna Williams. The painkillers that Dr. Hart recommended for you are also on the tray," said Toya. A hint of her Spanish accent coming out. She bowed her head in respect before leaving the room.

Tasha stared at the tray, and her tummy growled in anticipation. She was the type to eat a lot when she was upset.

Alpha Reid had realized that the night he had caught her trying to climb up the stairs with a stack of food in her hands. Ever since then, he made sure someone carried food to her room.

She walked over to the table and lifted the cover to see what the chefs had made for dinner. The sight of all the delicious food made her stomach rumble in excitement. Her face lit up with glee. They had made her favorite without knowing it. Fried drumsticks, barbeque wings, and rice and peas, with mashed potatoes and salad on the side.

Twenty minutes later, she was sitting in the chair like a bloated goat. Even though she had eaten until her belly was full, she had no regrets about overindulging.

Toya entered the room and saw Tasha sitting uncomfortably in the chair. She let out a joyous cackle at the sight. She had learned from her Alpha that Luna Williams ate a lot, her appetite rivaling that of a full-grown male wolf. At first, she had thought her Alpha was exaggerating. But when she saw it with her own eyes, she realized it was not a joke. She'd discovered the young Luna was quite a remarkable woman.

Chapter 33

Frustration swirled within Alexavier's depths as he tried to open his eyes. He felt like he was encased in a heavy fog, unable to move and unable to see anything but darkness. The wolf within him was on high alert, feeling his mate's distress. The sound of his mate's words lingered in his mind, as did the echo of her cries.

He was unaware of how long he had been like that. Unable to look at his mate's beautiful face. The memory of his fight with Dianna filled his head, bringing back a vivid reminder of the pain he felt in every muscle. He let out a pitiful whimper. He had failed to kill the woman that had hurt his mate. What good am I as an Alpha if I can't even protect the woman I was blessed with? He vowed he would rip Dianna to shreds if she was still alive when he woke up. The problem was, he didn't know when he would wake up.

Alexavier sighed in happiness when he started to feel the familiar tingles. He could feel his mate's body beside him, sending tingles up and down his side.

He summoned all his strength to force his eyes open. When the light from the room hit him, his lips curled up into a triumphant smile. He shielded his eyes from the bright, searing light and groaned.

His beast released a low, rumbling purr as a wave of tingles spread across his chest. He slowly removed his hand from his eyes and squinted, his gaze settling on his chest. His mate was snuggled up against him. One of her slender legs was thrown across his waist. His chest rose and fell rhythmically beneath her hand, which was unconsciously tracing circles.

Alexavier lifted his left hand, free from Tasha's grasp, and tenderly brushed the back of his knuckles against her cheek. A small smile formed on her lips as she leaned into his touch.

Her eyes flew open in shock as tingles danced across her cheek. Startled eyes met her mate's amused eyes. She lunged herself towards the man that had won her heart, her vision blurred by tears.

He cringed at the pain from the impact, but the warmth of his mate's embrace was enough to ease it away. As he felt her breaking down, he softly caressed her back in soothing circles. He breathed sweet words of reassurance into her ear. His voice was a gentle murmur to help stop her tears. His wolf whined in distress at the sight of his female's tears.

He pulled her closer to him and felt her body relax against him as her tears subsided. His wolf started purring as he felt her delicate fingers lightly trace the lines of his abdominal muscles. His lips formed a mischievous smirk. "Why do I get the feeling that you missed my abs more than me?"

Tasha slapped him lightly on his forehead. "I was checking your wounds to make sure you didn't rip the stitches."

"Sure, sure, use the wounds to cover up what you were actually doing," teased Alexavier. His laughter was deep and throaty as he took pleasure in teasing her.

She buried her face in the side of his neck, trying to hide her amusement. She was happy that he had woken up and didn't mind his teasing.

Her heart warmed at the feel of lips against her shoulder.

Alexavier's chest vibrated with a low, exasperated growl. His mate refused to let him leave the house for a run in his wolf form.

"You are not healed enough for that. What if the shift reopens the wound?" asked Tasha. Her eyes narrowed as she stared at him, refusing to back down.

Alexavier understood that his mate was just concerned about his wellbeing. But being cooped up in the house all day without releasing his wolf was driving him crazy. "Tasha, sweetheart, Dr. Hart already told us it's okay for me to change into my wolf. My stitches were removed and you've seen it for yourself that the wounds are basically nonexistent."

"You still need to rest, Alexavier. You were shot with damn silver bullets. Bullets that almost killed you. You almost died in my arms," she whispered. As she looked at her hands, remembering how they were covered in his blood.

He gently tugged her closer, and his muscular hands encircled her waist. The vacant and hopeless look in her eyes unnerved him. He pulled away from their embrace a bit to place a gentle kiss on her forehead. "Love, my wolf needs to run free. I haven't let him out since the battle and it's hard to keep him caged up for so long," said a determined Alexavier.

Tasha sighed, her shoulders slumping in defeat, knowing he was right. "Go ahead. I won't try to stop you." She removed herself from his embrace and walked out of the room they shared.

Alexavier grumbled to himself. He had a feeling that his mate was mad at him. So, he promised himself that he would make it up to her after his run. He needed to let his wolf out before they went home later that day.

Tasha sat on the steps at the front of the pack-house. She had already packed their things for their nighttime departure. She was ready to return home and reunite with her puppy, Zeus.

Tasha sensed him the moment he neared the tree line. Even if the dark woods concealed his form, she knew he had just returned from his run. She could feel his intense stare on her face, but she refused to acknowledge him. Knowing she had overreacted.

Whenever she was worried about someone special to her, she had a tendency to be overly dramatic. Although it was a reasonable response, it left her feeling embarrassed afterwards.

Alexavier put on the basketball shorts he had left near a tree. He then strode confidently towards where his mate was sitting. As he approached her, she got up and headed to the back of the house. Is she really that mad at me? He followed her from a distance.

Tasha stood in the backyard, staring into the darkness. Her mind filled with all things, Alexavier. The fear of the world she was introduced to being just another figment of her imagination weighed heavily on her mind. She was completely and utterly in love with Alexavier Blu. But the thought of waking up to find she was still all by herself filled her with dread.

A dream like this would leave my heart shattered.

She was so lost in her thoughts that she was oblivious to the sound of his footsteps approaching her. A startled shriek escaped her when she heard him clear his throat. She slowly turned to face her mate, who was less than a breath away from her.

"Is there a reason my mate is hiding and avoiding me in a dark place?" asked Alexavier, as he placed a hand on her cheek. His other hand rested on her waist, pulling her flush against him.

"I wasn't hiding. I just needed time to think about this new world I've entered... I don't want it to be a dream." She moved her hands from her sides and intertwined her fingers around his neck.

He leaned down and brushed his nose against hers, feeling the warmth of her breath on his face. "Believe me, Love, it's not a dream. This is all real. I'm very much real." He leaned in and placed a gentle kiss on the tip of her nose.

"You sure that's all there is to it, my little mate?" His eyes were full of questions, yet his mouth remained unyielding.

"Well, there is something else," she whispered. Her eyes glinted with a hint of mystery.

"Hmm and that is?" He inquired while his lips caressed her cheek. His wolf was purring harder than a pleased cat.

"I can show you better than I can tell you." She tightened her hands around his neck.

His eyes twinkled in amusement at her words. A deep rumble rose in his chest in anticipation. "What is it you would...?" His words died in his throat when he felt her soft lips pressed against his. The tenderness of her kiss told him all he needed to know; he could feel her love. As he bent his neck further to deepen their kiss, his growl of pleasure reverberated through his chest.

Tasha let out a low, satisfied moan. If this was another dream, she did not want to wake up.

His kiss was like a spark, igniting her nerve endings with a rush of excitement. Her toes curled in pure bliss.

Chapter 34

Tasha smiled as she approached the Alpha that had helped to rescue her. "Alpha Reid, thank you for all that you have done for us in the last couple of days. Sorry if we were any kind of inconvenience to your daily life."

Alpha Reid let out a deep, hearty chuckle while shaking his head. "Miss Williams, we have not had this much excitement in our lives in a while. It was a delight having you here and being able to assist you. You weren't an inconvenience, either."

Tasha stepped back after hugging the older Alpha.

Alexavier walked over to Alpha Reid after placing their bags in the SUV. He shook the older Alpha's hand. "Thank you again for helping us. Let me know if you require our help in the future."

"I'll keep that in mind. I wish you guys a safe journey. The guards will escort you out," said Alpha Reid. His smile mirrored the one on Tasha's face. He had grown quite fond of the little Luna in a paternal way.

Tasha and Alexavier waved goodbye to the rest of the group that had also shown up to send them off.

Alexavier had told his Beta to prepare for them to arrive before daybreak. He had the perfect plan set up to surprise his mate once they got back.

Tasha relaxed in the passenger seat of the SUV, smiling at how much her life had changed. She glanced at the man beside her and her lips curled into a wider smile. He wasn't just a dream anymore; he was real and her soulmate. She watched as his lips twitched, as if he was fighting back a smile. "What?"

"Oh nothing, just wondering why you're staring at me while smiling like a happy pit bull." His lips curved up in a playful smirk.

She giggled, her eyes crinkling with delight. "Am I not allowed to look at what's mine whenever I want?" She heard a deep, throaty rumble coming from his chest, and her lips twitched with amusement.

He liked the possessive note in her voice. His wolf started panting like a horny teenage pup.

Tasha watched as he bit his lip and she wished she was the one doing the biting. She absent-mindedly ran her tongue across her lips.

"Love, if you keep looking at me like that, I will not be responsible for what happens next," Alexavier growled out. The urge to pull the car over and let his mate have her way with him was driving him mad.

She squeezed her thighs together as she imagined the things she wanted him to do to her. The image of his lips caressing every inch of her body made her wet.

Alexavier let out a low growl. He could smell her arousal. Her intoxicating scent had the wolf within him, panting heavily. He pulled the car over to the side of the road and unfastened her seatbelt after doing the same to his. He lifted Tasha with a jolt, causing her to gasp as he settled her on his lap.

She moaned, her eyes closing at the feel of his bulge pressed against her heat. She was happy she'd worn leggings instead of jeans.

Even though she was straddling him in a car on the side of a dark road, it did nothing to diminish her burning desires.

Alexavier lost all rational thoughts when he heard her moan. He raised her chin using his index finger. His lips captured hers and he smiled, loving her immediate response. He groaned in ecstasy when he felt her rock against him. As he pulled away, his lips left a tingling sensation on hers as he placed a trail of kisses from her cheek to her neck.

Tasha felt a pleasant shudder ripple through her body. She gasped as his lips pressed against the area between her neck and shoulder. His lengthened canines grazed the area, and a deep, blissful sound escaped her lips. She tilted her head back, giving him more access.

He pressed his throbbing bulge against her heat, feeling her respond by grinding against him. Her movements snapped his remaining self-control. He licked the area he wanted to place his mark before sinking his fangs into her skin. Marking her as his. He growled possessively at the sweet sounds she let out. His fangs retracted, and he lapped at the blood on her neck.

She was so caught up in the feel of his lips against her skin. The pain she felt from his teeth sinking into her skin took her by surprise. But the pleasure she felt a few seconds after left her wanting him deep inside her. Her eyes slowly opened when she felt him tense. However, before she could question him, her world went dark.

Alexavier exhaled heavily as he gently lowered his mate into the passenger seat. He reached over to put her seatbelt on. "Stupid, stupid, stupid," he mumbled to himself while banging his head against the steering wheel. "How could you mark her without asking her first? Now she's going to hate you," he whispered.

His heart fell at the thought of his mate hating him. He gave her a lingering glance before the car's headlights illuminated the road ahead and he pulled back out onto the road. The sound of the engine hummed as he drove for another hour. He felt a knot in his stomach as he waited for her to wake up.

When Tasha opened her eyes, she felt dizzy and disoriented, eliciting a groan of discomfort. As she recalled the events that led to her pain, her body tensed and she froze in her seat. She couldn't believe Alexavier had finally marked her. She dreamt about it so many times, but didn't know what it meant.

It had slipped her mind to ask him the meaning behind a werewolf marking his mate. Now that he marked her, she felt more in tune with him. Even the sensation of his emotions was much more intense. She felt a mischievous grin spread across her face as a plan formed in her mind.

Chapter 35

Alexavier watched as her eyes opened slowly. He could feel her confusion, but he was too terrified to open his mouth. He was already sweating at the thought of her being mad at him.

"What did you do?" she asked with an arched brow.

"I... I... Uh... I have no idea what you mean," he stuttered out. He kept his eyes firmly on the road, refusing to even glance in her direction.

Although Tasha was internally filled with laughter, her expression remained neutral. She could feel how stressed out he was just by her question.

"Why did you bite me, Alexavier Blu?" she asked slowly.

Alexavier's sweat was dripping off his forehead like raindrops on a window. "Well, um, when a werewolf meets his or her mate, the male marks their female. So that other wolves know who that person belongs to. Normally it happens the minute a wolf meets their mate, but with humans, we try to follow human tradition," he answered.

He chanced a glance in her direction. "I know I should have explained it to you first, but I lost control back there. I don't regret doing it, though. However, I will apologize for not telling you beforehand. Now that you're bearing my mark, our emotions will be a lot more in tune. We will feel each other's pain, so if you get hurt anywhere on your body, I will know. I can hear your thoughts and talk to you through the mind-link too, unless you block me out. The mating is complete when we make love. Your scent will mix with mine and your senses will be a lot more enhanced. But that's if you still want me."

Tasha couldn't help but erupt in laughter, her body shaking with each chortle. Her big bad Alpha mate looked like a little kid that was caught stealing a cupcake from the pantry.

Alexavier thought his mate would reject him after he had explained. He was shocked by the sound of her laughter, bubbly and carefree, like a stream. Her reaction confused him. He glanced at her with a raised eyebrow.

She saw the confusion on his face and decided to ease his mind. "I dreamt of you marking me a few times. Though I didn't understand what it symbolized. But I noticed that all the mated females bore marks. I wondered why you never brought it up." She smiled at him and watched as his face relaxed.

His joy was evident, and her smile widened.

They entered their territory just before three in the morning. Alexavier heard the distinct sound of something moving in the woods and slowed the car down.

Tasha tensed as she scanned the darkness. Even though Alexavier tried to be subtle with his movements. She had noticed how alert he had become. She screamed in terror as something flew out of the shadows of the woods. It rammed into the side of the car before returning to the woods.

He pulled the car over to inspect the damage on the car. His wolf was on high alert and ready for a fight. He sniffed the air, trying to pick up how many wolves surrounded them.

"What the fuck are you doing?" she whispered. Her eyes continued to scan the area. She couldn't see too far out in the dark, but she could see things a lot clearer than other humans.

Alexavier raised his hand, signaling her to be quiet. He turned his head to the sound of light but fast-approaching footsteps.

Tasha started mumbling to herself. "I can't catch a break, can I? I just left one fight a few days ago to end up in another."

He motioned for her to get out of the car. He watched her silently creep out, and he stood ready to shield her from any danger.

Dane crouched in the tree, his mouth twitching as he observed his Luna below. For a woman who wasn't scared to take on rogues. She looked like she was having a hard time being out in the dark. He waited for his Alpha's signal.

When he spotted Alexavier's slight nod, he mind-linked his sister to release Zeus.

Tasha hated the dark with a passion. She wanted to slap Alexavier when he stopped the car instead of continuing driving. Actually, she wanted to strangle the man standing protectively in front of her. Her thoughts froze when she heard fast paws coming at them. She positioned herself for a fight but screamed when Alexavier stepped out of the way and something jumped on her.

She was still screaming even as she held whatever had attacked them. She felt a wet tongue lick at her cheeks and her eyes shot wide open. When she realized it was Zeus, her beloved puppy, she was filled with happiness and her laughter filled the air.

Alexavier chuckled at his mate's reaction. As soon as she was no longer paying attention, he gave another signal, and the pack emerged from the woods.

Tasha tensed, feeling a chill that sent shivers down her spine as the sound of many heartbeats pounded in the woods. She didn't know how big the threat was as stood staring into the darkness.

Growls vibrated the ground, and she quickly placed Zeus in the car before rushing back to her mate's side. "Please tell me you called for backup," she said through their mental connection. Without reinforcement, she didn't know how they would survive so many wolves.

The first wolf lunged, and she sent a roundhouse kick its way.

Dane whimpered, not expecting such strength behind his Luna's kick.

Tasha's eyes widened when she realized who she had kicked. She had never seen him in wolf form, but the familiar amber color told her it was Dane. The sound of his muffled whimpers filled her with panic. She wanted to check on him, but the sight of all the pack members emerging from the trees kept her rooted.

It was a mixture of different sized and colored wolves. They all bowed in unison, their heads lowered in reverent greeting to their Alpha and Luna.

Her heart swelled at the sight of her new family. Her eyes were glossy with tears that threatened to spill over—she was finally home. She walked over to Dane and hugged him. "I'm so sorry. I will give Alexavier a beating because I know this was his doing."

She ran her hand through his black fur before walking over to her mate.

Tasha's brown eyes were warm with love as she looked up at her man. "I love you, Alexavier Blu."

As he looked into her eyes, a wide smile spread across his face, and he tenderly placed his hand on her cheek. His eyes glowed gold when he said, "I love you with my whole being, my Love."

Alexavier spent a few days dealing with his company and pack's paperwork. The stack of papers wasn't too bad thanks to his parents, Gamma and Beta. However, he still had to look over the paperwork for his company.

He heaved a long sigh when he heard a knock on his office door. He inhaled, recognizing the familiar scent of his mate. His mate had made it her duty to remind him they still needed to deal with the people being held in the prison cells. "Come on in, Love."

Tasha pushed open the office door and joyfully skipped her way in, the door giving a loud bang as it swung shut behind her. Her lips pulled up into a serene grin. "Are you done with the paperwork? Do you need my help?"

"I was just finishing up. Do you need anything?" He already knew why she had entered his office. This was now a routine for them.

Her smile widened. "Well, we need to go deal with Dianna and her brother. I can punish them myself if you're busy with alpha duties."

He groaned and ran his hands over his tired face. "Baby girl, we've already talked about this. I can deal with those two myself. You don't need to get your pretty hands dirty."

Alexavier followed his mate, who was happily skipping her way towards the prison building. His stubborn mate had won their little battle. All it took was for her to remind him he had marked her without her consent. His queen had also threatened to withhold hugs and kisses if he didn't allow her to help punish Dianna and Dave.

The prison guards greeted them.

Tasha and Alexavier followed the guards, who led them to the first cell which contained Dianna.

The soft jingle of keys outside her cell caused Dianna's head to raise slightly. She couldn't help but smirk when the two people entered, but she kept her snide remarks to herself. As much as she wanted to latch her canine teeth into Tasha's neck, she remained seated in her corner.

"What's wrong Dianna, has your book of bitching run out of words?" Tasha taunted. The corners of her lips tugged upward, her smirk barely visible.

Dianna growled, her lips pulled back to reveal sharp teeth, but she stayed seated. She did not have the energy to attack the human in front of her or the Alpha that watched her like a true predator. She had refused to eat and drink what the guards had offered her.

"How's your little brother? Is he as chatty as he was when you guys had me locked up?" Asked Tasha. She rubbed her chin as if she was thinking. "He will join your mate and your best friend soon."

Those words made Dianna lose her composure. Her wolf rose to the surface, snarling at the mention of her dead mate. She wanted blood, specifically the human's blood.

Alexavier tensed, but his mate stood there unbothered.

Tasha was going to give the bitch exactly what she deserved for kidnapping her and hurting her mate. She felt the warmth of her mate's chest as she leaned back against him. She met the woman's icy stare with a deadly gaze of her own. "I would have let you live if you had just let me go. Yet you were determined to kill me. Your biggest mistake was kidnapping me and not killing me on the spot."

She shook her head. "No, your downfall was thinking that all humans are weak minded. You should remember that some of us have a reason to survive just like you."

Alexavier growled his displeasure at her statements. He wrapped a hand protectively around her waist.

"Guards!" called Tasha.

The two men approached the cell and bowed to their Luna. "What can we do for you, Luna?" They asked in unison.

"Take her to the fighting area and watch her until I get there."

The two guards raised their heads, surprised by their Luna's request. They stared at their Alpha for his approval.

Tasha quirked a brow at the two guards. "That was an order!"

The two men hurried over to unlock the chain from around Dianna's ankle. They each grabbed one of her hands and pulled her from the cell.

Dianna growled and screamed curses at them while being dragged out of the prison.

Alexavier shook his head in amusement. Even now, his mate was willing to give the evil woman a fair fight.

Tasha turned in his arms and kissed him on the lips. "I'll leave you to deal with the other one." She smiled sweetly at him before walking out of the prison.

Alexavier walked out of Dianna's cell and headed over to the one that Dave occupied. Unlike his mate, he didn't have time for games. He smirked at Dave, who started whimpering just by his mere presence. He knew his eyes showed his wolf was present.

Before Dave could blink, his Alpha was a foot away from him. He attempted to scramble away, fear making his movements jittery.

With a single, powerful motion, Alexavier effortlessly lifted him from the ground. "I hope you enjoy hell, traitor," he whispered in a deadly voice. His claws grew, and he used his free hand to rip out Dave's spinal cord.

He dropped the lifeless body before signaling for the guards to clean it up. He left the prison, eager to watch his mate fight.

He returned to his room, where he took a quick shower. He pulled on a pair of sweatpants before making his way toward the fighting grounds.

Chapter 36

Tasha stood facing Dianna on the field, the air thick with the pack's hushed anticipation. She had brought the steel baseball bat that Dane had gifted her. She had coated the bat with silver after he told her it was her new weapon. When she remembered the day, he gave her the bat; she let out a loud, hearty laugh.

Dane had approached her with something behind his back. It was securely wrapped. "Hey Luna, do you have a minute?"

"Hey, how many times do I have to tell you to just call me Tasha? What can I help you with?"

He cracked a broad smile that lit up his face. "I have something for you. I know how much you like using a branch as a weapon of choice. But it doesn't last long in a fight." He handed her the object. "Hopefully, this will be a better weapon."

Tasha's face beamed with excitement when she was given the gift. As she unwrapped her gift, her smile grew bigger. "OMG! I love this Dane. Thank you!"

Tasha was brought back to her current situation when she felt tingles on her cheek. She opened her eyes to see her mate standing in front of her with worry in his eyes. "My bad, I zoned out for a minute."

Alexavier's hand dropped from her cheek. "You better end this fight without a scratch on you or else."

"Or else what?" she asked. A cheeky smile playing on her lips.

He stepped closer to her and whispered in her ear. "Or else I'll assign guards to you whenever you step out of the house."

Her mouth fell open as she watched him walk away with a satisfied smirk on his lips. "As if I would let you have your way," she grumbled.

"Let's get this over with," said Tasha to a glaring Dianna.

The two females circled each other. Dianna attacked first, sending a roundhouse kick to Tasha's cheek.

Tasha flew back from the force of the kick; landing on her butt. Despite the sting in her butt and cheek, she quickly got back on her feet.

Alexavier's chest rumbled with a deep, threatening growl. His wolf rose to the surface, but he stood rooted. He knew if he made a move to help his mate, she would give him hell.

Tasha watched as the woman approached her, with a look on her face that could give Satan a run for his money. She gripped the bat in her hand and waited for Dianna to make her move.

Dianna punched with her left hand, and Tasha used the bat to block. She hissed as the silver burned her hand. A low growl fell from her lips as she aimed a kick at Tasha's head.

Tasha ducked just in time and sent an uppercut to Dianna's chin.

Dianna fell on her bottom a good distance from Tasha. She hurriedly got up as Tasha closed the distance. She readied herself as Tasha ran at her.

She stepped back when Tasha swung the bat and Dianna sent a left hook to the side of her face.

Tasha hissed and spit out blood. She ducked as Dianna swept her lengthened claws at her.

She spun out of the way as Dianna tried to sweep her off her feet. She stopped a punch with the bat and kicked Dianna in the stomach.

Dianna doubled over in pain, and Tasha grabbed her hair.

Tasha's knee collided with her face before she could block it. Dianna's head snapped back, and she fell to the ground.

Tasha stood back, trying to catch her breath as she waited for Dianna to get up. She noticed the sluggishness of Dianna's reflexes, and how her speed was far behind her usual pace.

"Kill her Luna!" the pack members shouted.

Tasha paid them no mind. She had her own plans for the cruel woman.

Dianna snarled at the pack that had once been her family. With a deep breath, she rose from the ground. She felt a throbbing sensation in her head due to the strength behind the punch. But she refused to die at the hands of a mere human who had already taken everything from her. She released her control, giving her wolf free rein.

Tasha watched the wolf carefully. She didn't dare underestimate the wolf with a missing paw. She stood with her feet planted shoulders-width apart and both hands gripping the bat as the wolf lunged at her.

Dianna felt a sense of confusion as she looked at the other woman, who stood motionless. Her jaws opened, showing her razor-sharp teeth as she aimed to rip Tasha's head from her body.

Tasha spun out of the way at the last second and swung the bat into the side of the wolf. She used a lot of strength, so it did not surprise her when the wolf whimpered. A giggle fell from her lips as she watched pack members dive out of the way.

Dianna's body felt like it was on fire from the silver. She closed her eyes as she felt the wind rushing through her fur as she sailed through the air and crashed into a tree. There was a loud crack when she hit the tree and her whines filled the air. Her body fell to the ground with a thud. She was in pain all over and the weakness from her not eating had fully kicked in as the adrenalin left her.

Tasha strode confidently towards Dianna, with Alexavier almost glued to her heels. She noticed the female was barely breathing. She turned to face her mate. "Get someone else to finish her." She honestly didn't want someone else's blood on her.

Alexavier signaled for one of his pack warriors to do the job. He swooped his mate into his arms and carried her to the pack-house. "You fought well, my beautiful Luna," he whispered as he placed her feet on the floor.

He kissed her forehead. "Go take a shower. I'm going to make sure everything regarding Dianna is over."

Tasha smiled at him. She could tell that his wolf was still close to the surface. The gold in his eyes glinted fiercely. She wrapped her hands around his neck and pulled his head closer.

When their lips met, his chest rumbled in pleasure and she felt a smile tugging at her lips. She pulled back after biting his lips and rushed to the bathroom. A smile of pure joy tugged at the corners of her mouth.

Alexavier growled his displeasure as he stared at the closed door. He shook his head and chuckled at his mate's teasing as he left their room. He loved and enjoyed the way she teased him.

Tasha let out an exasperated groan and smacked her forehead with her palm. She had forgotten her clothes while running from her mate. Wrapped in her towel, she stood close to the bathroom door, listening for any movements in the bedroom. She sighed as her shoulders relaxed when she heard no sound from her mate.

She made her way to their shared walk-in closet. She hurriedly looked through her clothes, trying to pick out something to wear. Knowing that her mate could arrive at any second.

The hairs on the back of her neck stood on end as the door to their bedroom opened. Before she could even think of turning and running to the bathroom, she could feel her mate's presence right behind her. She gasped as he ran a finger up her exposed thighs.

"Do you enjoy teasing me, mate?" he whispered against her ear. He placed a gentle kiss against her shoulder and ran his tongue over a droplet of water running down her neck.

She shuddered, her hands trembling as she tightened her grip on the towel. Her eyes rolled to the back of her head as his hands made their way to her heated core. His hand stopped a few inches away and her eyes shot open.

"Answer me!" he demanded and kissed her mark. His voice was a low growl that sent shivers down her spine.

Her knees buckled at the sensation of his lips against her mark. She could barely think, much less form a sensible sentence. "No...

I... I... forgot my....." Her words died as pleasurable moans replaced them.

Alexavier rubbed his finger against her sensitive flesh. He separated her folds and hover his finger over her entrance. "I'm waiting for your answer, my Love," he growled out. His breathing was labored as he struggled to control himself. He wanted nothing more than to worship his mate's body.

He was willing to take his time tasting and teasing every inch of her. His dick twitched at the thought of entering his mate's warmth. He could already feel her juice dripping on his finger.

"I... I... do," she finally gasped out. She threw her head back as sensual cries passed her lips. His finger had entered her dripping sex. Her grip on the towel loosened, and it fell to the floor.

Alexavier growled possessively at his mate's naked body. She was beautiful; a masterpiece that belonged to him. He ran his free hand over every dip and curve before gripping her freed breast. He kneed one bud before moving to the next. His dick was throbbing as her sweet sounds of ecstasy filled the room. He added another finger, stroking and scissoring inside her.

As her hips moved to match his rhythm. He wrapped his free hand around her throat as he increased the speed of his pumping. His lips brushed her ears as he growled, "So tight, so wet and all, MINE!"

"Alexavier!" she screamed out as she hit her climax.

He tightly embraced her as she collapsed into his chest, her body shaking from her orgasm.

"Turn around, Love," he whispered.

She turned to face him; her gaze smoldering with a mix of lust and love. His chest vibrated with a satisfied rumble. He swept her off her feet into his arms and carried her to the bed. He placed her down on the bed with gentle care before removing his pants and boxer.

He puffed out his chest as her eyes traveled the length of his body. His lips curled into a satisfied smirk as her eyes widened at the size of his dick.

He gripped his dick in his palm as he watched her spread her legs wide. Her pussy glistened, begging for him to enter.

She bit her lip and her fingers gripped the sheets as she stared at the length of his dick. She was nervous but excited to be fully mated to him. But she was not looking forward to the pain.

Her worries were put to rest as he took his time with her. Every touch and stroke was gentle.

Their night was filled with the sounds of pleasure and passionate embraces.

Epilogue

6 Months Later

Tasha rose from her slumber to her body flushed against her mate's naked chest. Her heart warmed as she gazed at the serene expression on his face.

They had made love right through the night. The soreness between her legs served as a reminder that they had been going at it like two rabid animals.

She grabbed her phone to check the time. Her best friend was visiting her for the first time since she moved away. She was buzzing with excitement about finally reuniting with Jade for the weekend.

She carefully shifted Alexavier's arm from around her waist and got up from the bed. She snatched her robe off the floor; the material rustled against her skin as she covered her nakedness. She opened her room door and Zeus entered, his tail wagging excitedly. "Good morning, my handsome boy," she greeted the husky affectionately as he showered her with puppy kisses.

Tasha walked into the bathroom and gazed at her reflection in the mirror. The mark on her neck looked more like two beauty spots than a bite mark. The person looking back at her in the mirror was wearing a huge Cheshire cat grin.

She recalled how the pack had thrown a huge celebration to honor their new Luna and Alpha's mating. Her lips curled into a smile at the fond memory.

She did her usual morning routine in the bathroom. She had a few more hours to go before she needed to collect Jade from the airport. When Tasha opened the bathroom door, she saw her mate smiling and holding a steaming cup of tea for her. She beamed with gratitude, "thank you, Love."

"You're welcome, baby girl. I'm going to freshen up so we can go have breakfast."

While Alexavier was in the bathroom, Tasha got dressed. She wore a white long-sleeve crop top, blue high-waist jeans. Perfectly offset by her white combat boot, perfect for the cool, fall air. She reached for her trusty leather jacket and her favorite black purse. She told Zeus to follow her as she sauntered out of her bedroom.

In the kitchen, she poured out Zeus's food into his bowl and handed it to him. "I'll be taking you to get groomed next week," she said to the dog, who was busy devouring his food.

Zeus had grown a great deal, and his fur had formed tight knots. Even though she combed through it every other day.

A shriek of surprise escaped her lips when Alexavier blew air on her neck. When she turned to hit him, her arm froze in midair as she took in the sight of his clothing. He looked downright delicious in his outfit.

His white button-down shirt showed off his toned muscles, and the four buttons that he left undone gave her a peek of his delicious pecs. The dark blue jeans he wore fit snugly against his powerful thighs. He finished the look with a pair of white Air Force 1.

Tasha's dry lips parted as her tongue darted out to moisten them. Her man belonged in the sexiest man alive magazine. Her eyes drank in every detail as they made their way up to his eyes. His eyes glowed their beautiful gold as he took in her outfit. "I'm starting to think you like matching with me," she said with a smug smirk.

As he took slow steps towards her, she was rewarded with the sound of his deep, resonating chuckle. He wrapped his arms around her petite body. "I don't see a problem with me matching the most stunning woman in the world." He leaned down and gently pressed his lips to hers.

He softly bit her lip, asking for entry. She granted him access, and his tongue explored her mouth, eliciting a sensual moan from her. He slowly pulled away from the kiss, leaving her lips feeling warm and tingly.

"Are you ready?"

"Yes, let's go," she said breathlessly.

His fingers intertwined with hers as they left her apartment. They had breakfast at a diner. Their regular pancakes, eggs, bacon, sausages, and hash browns with orange juice.

After breakfast, they met up with Dane, who joined them to pick up Jade.

Tasha shifted in her seat restlessly as they waited for Jade to come out of the airport. Her excitement made the men laugh.

Alexavier couldn't help but grin as his mate's eyes lit up with happiness. He knew how much she had missed her best friend. He looked up at the rearview mirror to see his brother staring out the window with a small smile on his lips.

The moment Tasha saw Jade, she flung the car door open, eager to greet her. She ran and embraced the smaller woman in a tight hug. She threw her head back and laughed as people gawked at them. "Oh, how I've missed you," she said, smiling from ear to ear.

"Well, you shouldn't have moved so far then. I'm starting to think you moved away because you were tired of me," Jade replied with a playful pout.

Tasha rolled her eyes as she stepped away from the only family she had left after her parent's death. "Yeah, right, I told you to come with me countless times before the move."

Jade's laughter filled the air as she shrugged her shoulders. "I can't recall." Her gaze locked on the two tall, dark and handsome men coming towards them, their silhouettes standing out against the crowd. Her eyes roamed their frame, taking in every detail. She couldn't believe she was missing out on such fine men while living in New Jersey. She cleared her throat with a raspy sound. "Um, sis, are those men with you?"

Tasha spun around to face the direction her best friend was staring. She giggled, her eyes twinkling as they met Alexavier, who in response raised his eyebrow in a silent question.

"Yes, they are. The one whose outfit matches mine is Alexavier. You've talked to him on the phone a few times. He is my boyfriend."

Jade's eyes widened in surprise as her jaw dropped open. "Girl! That phone did not do that man justice. He is gorgeous."

Tasha let out a light, tinkling laugh. "Tell me about it. The next gentleman is his brother Dane."

Jade licked her lips as she stared at Dane. "Is he single? I'd like to have a taste of him."

Dane let out an incredulous sputter at Jade's statement. He was not expecting her to be so straightforward.

Tasha hit Jade in the back of her head. "Please behave," she whispered as the men finally came to a stop in front of them.

"Hi Jade, nice to finally meet you in person," Alexavier greeted.

Jade turned to her best friend with wide eyes. "Damn, his voice is really deep. My phone speaker was actually working properly," she whispered.

Tasha smacked her palm against her forehead as Alexavier's chuckle filled her head.

"Nice to meet you too," Jade greeted with a Cheshire grin. She turned to Dane, "hello, dear handsome. Are you single?"

Dane smiled shyly at the small, self-assured woman. "Hi, I'm Dane. Nice to meet you. I'm free as a bird the last time I check."

Tasha grabbed Jade by the shoulder as she noticed the danger-ous smirk making its way onto her face. "You will not do what you are thinking of doing," she warned as she steered her towards the car.

She shouted to the two men standing with bewildered looks on their faces. "Can one of you bring her suitcase?"

"So Dane, will you be staying the night at my sis's place, too?" asked Jade. She was sitting next to him in the car as they made their way to Tasha's home.

Tasha groaned at her best friend's question. "Please leave the man alone. I am begging."

Alexavier chuckled next to her. His eyes focused on the road, but he could feel how embarrassed she was. "It's okay, Love. Dane can handle her," he tried to reassure her through their link.

"No. I'll be heading home with my brother once we drop you ladies off," answered Dane. The woman was straightforward, and he liked that about her. However, he had a mate out there, and having a good time with his sister-in-law's best friend was a no−no.

She stuck her bottom lip out in a pout. Her dark eyes were wide with innocence. "That's such a shame."

Alexavier and Dane made sure the ladies were settled before heading home.

"Jade is quite interesting," said Alexavier, as he drove to the pack-house.

Dane sighed and shook his head in disbelief. "Tell me about it. I was not expecting that at all. She is the complete opposite of our Luna. But they complement each other so well."

Alexavier grinned, "that they do."

Tasha spent the weekend showing her bestie all the fun places she had been to while living in Ferryville. They chatted about everything and nothing. Their nights were spent on her couch watching romantic movies. Zeus was stretched across them like a blanket.

"Still can't believe Dane did not want this," Jade said to her when she was leaving.

Tasha hugged her. "It's not that he doesn't. It's more like he can't."

Jade pulled away, her mouth wide open in disbelief. "Don't tell me he fancies the same tool as us."

Tasha burst out laughing. "No, more like an arranged marriage."

"What?! Black Americans do such things?" She asked in shock.

"I guess so," said Tasha. She bit her lips to keep from laughing at the ridiculous face her best friend was making.

"That's a shame. Well, I better get going before I miss my flight. Tell the guys bye for me and I'll call you when I land," said Jade. She gave her bestie one last hug.

Tasha waved goodbye to her best friend, her vision blurred with tears. "I will."

She pulled her ringing phone from her pocket and chuckled at the caller ID. "I'm fine, Love. I was just telling Jade bye," she answered.

"I know Love. Turn around," Alexavier replied.

Tasha turned to face her mate with shock written all over her face. "What are you doing here?" she asked as he approached her.

"I came to check on you, to make sure you weren't crying your eyes out while standing on the street." He chuckled as she turned away to wipe her tears.

"Who is crying?" she asked, while hugging herself.

Alexavier pulled her into his chest. Hugging her tight, he enjoyed the feeling of their bodies interlocking like a perfect puzzle piece. He gazed into her warm brown eyes. Her eyes sparkled with love for him. He leaned in to capture her lips to show her just how much he loved and adored her.

"I love you more," they said in unison through their shared link.